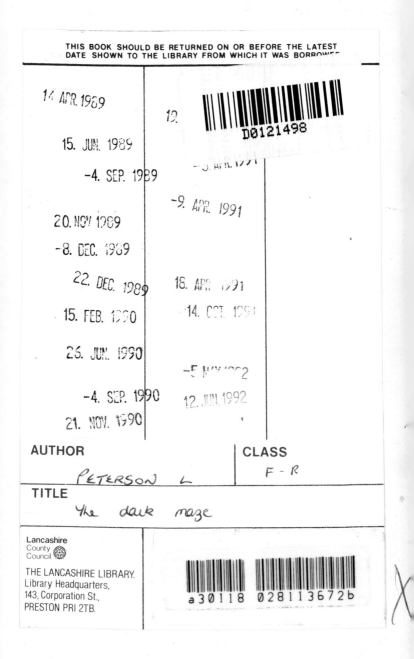

AUTHOR

PETERSON   L

CLASS

F - R

TITLE

The dark maze

THE DARK MAZE

ALSO IN THE SERIES

THE DARK MAZE

Lito Peterson

A *Troubadour*
Edited by Lesley Saxby

MACDONALD AND JANE'S . LONDON

First published in Great Britain in 1978 by
Macdonald & Jane's Publishers Ltd
Paulton House
8 Shepherdess Walk
London N 1

17809963
028113672
LAST COPY
SA

ISBN 0 354 04187 8

Printed and bound in Great Britain by
REDWOOD BURN LIMITED
Trowbridge and Esher

To my sister
Marie

CHAPTER ONE

Mexico City was not as I had expected it to be. I had done a little home-work and imagined, vaguely, that it would have something of the style of its early Aztec origins. An absurd notion. It was, of course, a busy, thriving, modern city. As I gazed, a little disconsolately, out of my hotel bedroom window on to the broad avenues, well-designed hotels and buildings and the eternal traffic, I saw the grey man again. He stood on the opposite side of the road, waiting to cross over to my hotel's side. He was wearing the same grey wind jacket with grey trousers. His hair was grey-black and his dark, thin face hardly registered in all that greyness. All the same, there was a peculiar clarity about his eyes, when, perhaps drawn by my stare, he looked up seemingly straight at my window. I caught a glint of the sun in them and instinctively drew back out of his view. It was odd that a perfect stranger should arouse such unease in me.

The first time I had noticed the man was on the previous day at the Anthropological Museum. A 'must', everyone who knew Mexico City had said. Dutifully, I had taken a taxi and went there to browse around on my own. My first day had been spent on a bus tour looking at a lot of boring churches and buildings. Not a rubber-neck by inclination, I yet felt compelled to 'do' a conducted tour of any town I visited for the first time;

1

afterwards I just drifted here and there by myself which was usually far more rewarding. Certainly I had not been disappointed in the Anthropological Museum. Architecturally exciting on the outside, the inside was full of interest too. The chronological history of the early Americans was set out with such graphic clearness, that even I, a mere anthropologically unaware solicitor, found it easy to follow. In fact, I stayed riveted for hours. Here were excellent model reproductions of the City as it had looked in all its splendour when the Spanish Conquistadores, led by Cortez, had first seen it. Believing him to be a god returned after a long absence, the Aztecs gave him a tremendous ovation, so that Cortez was overwhelmed, both by the magnificence of their country and his reception. Inevitably this uneasy honeymoon was of short duration; the Spaniards, greedy for the abundant gold, eventually turned on and brutally destroyed their hosts.

Some of the frightful things done in the name of the Inquisition were also shown. I turned away in disgust. Man's inhumanity to man always sickened me.

In the upstairs galleries were life-size models of present-day Indians, dressed in the colourful clothes of their various tribes. They were shown in groups busy at their tasks, in and around their homes. Not many people were here, so that turning from one of these groups of waxen figures, I immediately noticed the man in grey standing some way away from me in the long corridor, his tall, thin figure silhouetted against the large pane of glass at the end.

He was standing perfectly still and seemed to be staring at me. My first reaction was that he knew me, had met me on the tour perhaps, and I half raised my hand to wave an acknowledgement. But he did not wave back, just

2

went on staring through and beyond me. I turned round in surprise to see whether there was someone behind for whom he was waiting, but there was no one there; only the figures of the Indians, weaving, pounding maize, chopping wood and so on, in that strange frozen way wax figures have, as though bewitched in the midst of life. When I looked back again, puzzled, the man had vanished. Had I imagined him? I walked rapidly down the nearest staircase and out of the imposing building into the sunshine, unreasonably disturbed. Worse, my depression was back.

Obviously I had not imagined him, since here he was again. Perhaps he was staying in the hotel? But why associate him in my mind with Maria? Why should he intimidate and depress me? Straightening my tie, I prepared to go down to my newly-made American acquaintances, a middle-aged couple I had met on the tour.

They were waiting for me at the bar with friendly smiles.

'Hi, John,' I was greeted by the young-fifties husband. 'Meet my little sister, Babe Weimer. She came out to join us today. This is John Devigne.' The Americans' excellent habit of remembering a name always put me to shame. I could not remember theirs!

'How do you do,' I said.

'Hi,' Babe said. She was about my age, early thirties, bright blonde and bright-eyed. 'Just great,' she added, knocking back what looked like a Bloody Mary.

The wife of the American drew me a little to one side and said in a low voice, 'Babe lost her husband about three months ago. We asked her out here to forget.'

'I see. I'm sorry,' I answered solemnly and went to help her husband with the drinks.

We brought them over to the women, and Babe was

3

saying something while my mind was still wrestling
with the fixation I was developing about the grey man.

'Don't you think so, Mr Devigne? Or may I call you
John, if you call me Babe?' she was asking.

'Please do.' I smiled. 'But 'I'm afraid I missed your
question.'

'Why not eat at the restaurant where they have the
Flamenco dancers. It may be crowded, but I do love
Flamenco, don't you?'

'I don't know much about it,' I murmured. 'But I
should be delighted to go if that's what you would like.'

'Great,' she said again and went straight into an
account of her experiences with Flamenco dancers.

A real talker that one, I decided, listening to the flow
with only half an ear. How real was her sorrow, though?
Her late husband must have left her stashed, judging by
the rocks covering her fingers and the jangling bangles
also studded with stones. She even wore a slim diamond
bracelet round her ankle, on which was a ridiculous,
small, golden bell.

Seeing my glance travelling down to this, she
informed me, 'Yes, my husband gave me that. If you
want me, just ring, honey, he used to say. He was a
lovely man.' And she composed her features into a conventional mask of sorrow.

I gave up listening altogether after that. I could not
stand false sentiment. Women were prone to it. Not so
Maria; nothing phoney about *her* sentiments. She could
be tender with love or fiery with hate, but it all went
deep. I felt myself drowning with longing to be with her
again; heartsick, I longed for something now impossibly
out of reach.

Babe was pressing me again to answer her. I looked at
her questioningly, with raised brows. She burst out

laughing. 'I guess you're just the strong, silent type. But I like that. I talk for two anyway. Come on. We're on our way,' and she put her arm possessively through mine.

That was another thing I found irritating amongst so many women. If they decided they liked you, they instantly tried to possess you. No question of waiting to see first if you liked them too. I suffered her to lead me to the door where we all piled into a waiting taxi.

Babe relinquished my arm reluctantly and sat with her sister-in-law on the opposite side. Though I smiled automatically at her, my thoughts, as so often of late, switched into the past . . .

Maria had not been the pushing type. When I first kissed her, she had resisted, trembling. (Like that small bird I had picked up and held for comfort – its heart had beat so loudly as it shivered in my hand, I had had to put it down.)

Concerned, I had pleaded with her. 'What is it? Don't you like me? Are you frightened of me?'

'Yes. No, John. I do like you, but I'm frightened.' Her clear green eyes had clouded over and become opaque.

'Don't be frightened, Maria. I wouldn't hurt you for the world. I couldn't help kissing you – you are so beautiful.'

She had looked at me seriously for a moment, then broken into a smile, and with a faint shake of her head, walked away.

Elated, I remember hurrying out into the garden where my mother was sitting in her wheel chair doing her everlasting embroidery. Seizing the abandoned hoe, I had swung at the weeds, a sudden burst of song coming out of me. 'Gracious, John, must you? You are off key,'

5

my mother had protested in astonishment.

I had been over and over the sweetness and excitement of that first encounter many times since.

Reluctantly, I brought my mind back to the present. The taxi was just drawing up at the restaurant and we were soon found a small table in the crowded room, full of smoke and noise.

Babe did not seem to mind the smallness of the table. It gave her an excuse to sit close to me, her thigh pressing against mine and when she leaned over to talk to her sister-in-law on my other side, her breasts pressed against my arm. I looked at her speculatively. She was not my type, but she was sexy enough. I had not been to bed with a woman since Maria.

'Strong and silent' Babe had called me. Not outstandingly strong, though tennis in the summer and squash in the winter kept me fit and wiry with no bulge as yet. Silent, fairly, yes. Often catching in other people's remarks an echo of my own fatuousness, I had gradually over the years become more silent, shrinking from the small talk: the exaggerated enthusiasms, easy condemnations, complacency and clichés. I was not, however, silent all the time. When something interested me, I talked as much as anyone, almost with a sense of release. It had been like that with Maria; we talked together for hours, when we were not making love.

Still, it was no good thinking about that now.

I merely smiled at Babe, not finding anything to say. She did not seem to care. In fact, it appeared to excite her that I was silent. Her thigh felt hot under her thin dress and she was now openly making eyes at me. Probably the succession of Bloody Marys had also gone to her head.

'Would you like to dance?' I asked her.

'Too late,' she said. 'They are just announcing the Flamenco act.' She understood a little Spanish.

The Flamenco was very good. Feet stamped, the flounced skirts whirled, and the dancers became increasingly tense, tossing their heads haughtily, flinging their arms up in curved gestures, their fingers busy with the castanets. A girl came on who instantly reminded me of Maria. I was always seeking her image in others. I craned forward eagerly.

This girl was slim and graceful. She had the same black hair, high cheekbones and gleaming teeth – but there the resemblance ended. Her face lacked both the intelligence and sweetness of Maria's and her dark eyes looked sulky. All the same, she was a brilliant dancer. Fierce, vital, a ball of fire. We were spellbound and the crowded room became silent as the music died out, leaving her tapping, tapping, tapping, to the beat of her own castanets. She went on and on, like someone in a trance. It was almost unendurable to watch and I became increasingly exhausted and anxious for her, fearing she would drop down dead. Abruptly, she gave a final decisive clack of the castanets, her hands flung high, and stopped precisely in a graceful movement as though poised for flight. It was a *tour de force*. We were mesmerized and still, then I was clapping in a frenzy with the rest. I wanted to get to her, praise her, beg her to join us for a drink. She had for me some of the magic of Maria.

Babe was pressing heavily on me, saying, 'Wasn't she just great?' And I was suddenly back to earth.

It was hot. The spotlights and tension in the room had raised the temperature to an unbearable degree. The perspiration was rolling down my face. The combination of heat, emotion and a greasy omelette I had half eaten,

7

had upset me. Rising quickly, I said, 'I'm afraid I must ask you to excuse me. The heat has made me feel faint. The thin air up here seems to take me that way. I shall have to go outside.'

'It *is* too hot,' Babe said. 'Let's all go.'

'No, no,' I said urgently. 'I don't want to spoil your evening. May I settle with you tomorrow?' I asked the American.

'Please – you are my guest anyway.' They all seemed concerned rather than offended, so I must have looked pretty sick.

'Thank you. See you tomorrow,' I said, and fled.

Once outside, I quickly felt better, and decided to walk back to the hotel. The night air was cool and the City lights sparkled; at this height, they had a special brilliance. It was a relief to be alone with my thoughts. The Spanish dancer had aroused in me, not desire for women in general, but for Maria in particular. I knew the dancer was an illusion; a restless longing, an empty hope for a Maria replacement.

Arrived at the hotel, I thankfully took the lift to my room, had a shower, poured out a strong whisky and propped myself in bed to sip it slowly and indulge in dreams of the early, happy days with Maria. I had, unsuccessfully, tried to strifle all thoughts of her since leaving England. But the excitements of the day had forced the flood gates open and now I deliberately relaxed to let the memories come pouring out.

CHAPTER TWO

'Of course, she's a foreigner,' my mother had said to me on that Friday before her arrival. 'She's Greek, but her mother is English,' she added, as though this made it permissible for Maria to exist. 'Anyway, she was highly recommended by the Embassy family, the Plummers, where she has been these past two years – so I engaged her. She's due here tomorrow.'

'I'm glad you are getting a permanent again,' I said. 'These temporaries are a headache. You've no sooner got them trained than they're off.'

'You're telling me,' said my mother, who uses the idiom of her youth.

She is nearly seventy, crippled with arthritis, but still a bright, alert woman mentally. Her hands are well, so she is able to work on the embroidery she loves, but her hips and knee joints are so affected that she can only walk with great difficulty and is forced to use a wheel chair. That is why it is necessary for her to have a living-in help; a kind of companion-housekeeper. Needless to say, to find anyone to fill this post for any length of time is not easy. Though well paid, young girls quickly become bored with living in the country and older, nervier women, and sooner or later pick quarrels. Not that my mother is particularly difficult; she has humour and her remarks are pithy. Television and embroidery are her main occupations – but her real life is lived through me.

She and my father tried in vain for years to have a child and when at the age of thirty-five my mother was at last able to produce a healthy son, it seemed like a miracle to them and I suppose they doted on me. Four years later my father was killed on D Day. After that Mother brought me up virtually alone and we became devoted to each other. Fortunately, my father had left us both well provided for.

Though my solicitor's practice is in London, so that during the week I live in a flat overlooking Regent's Park, week-ends are spent with my mother in Suffolk. It is the least I can do. She is naturally possessive over me, which I accept cheerfully, or so I have always thought. Anyway, I enjoy working in the garden; she, too, had been a great gardener once, and the half-timbered house in its typical English setting is the kind of dream home one sees on calendars.

Why my basically broad-minded mother should adopt this suspicious attitude towards 'foreigners', I do not know. Devigne had once been 'de la Vigne'. My mother claims we came over with the Norman Conquest, so most likely my noble ancestor had been a peasant tilling his vines in France!

I said to her, continuing the conversation, 'But, darling, the best girl you ever had was Portuguese. She stayed nearly three years. Maybe this one will stick too.'

My mother sniffed a bit at mention of the Portuguese. Stout and strong and with a flourishing moustache, by the third year she reckoned she could run everything better than Mother – and the clash had come. She had left in a huff to marry a travelling salesman; maybe he found the moustache attractive.

Since then an agency had supplied a succession of

breezy, pleasant Australian and New Zealand 'temporaries', who were always on the wing to Canada or Hong Kong or anywhere but Suffolk. So poor Mother really felt the need of someone to settle again and I sincerely hoped this coming one would work out.

On the Saturday morning, the front door bell rang around 10.30. I was writing some letters in the study, my mother was in her chair in the garden, and Mrs Hoggs, our faithful daily from the village, was upstairs cleaning the bedrooms. So I cried, 'I'll go, Hugs,' and went to open the door.

A girl with long, black hair, a charming smile and the most beautiful luminous eyes I had ever seen, was standing there.

'Hallo,' I said, and waited to find out what she wanted.

'Hallo,' she answered. 'Is this Mrs Devigne's house? I'm Maria.,

'Maria who?' I asked stupidly.

'Too difficult. Never mind. Just call me Maria. I'm the new help.'

I was stunned. Where was the moustache, the stout figure, and thick foreign accent I had visualized? This was a slim, beautiful girl, who spoke perfect English.

It was April and I was suddenly aware of the sweetness of the spring day. A blackbird sang clearly – at least, I think it was a blackbird – and a certain enchantment came over me so that for a few seconds I did not move, just stood there, conscious of being alive, looking at Maria and, no doubt, smiling idiotically.

She bent to pick up her suitcase which I had not noticed and I came out of my daze.

'I'll take that upstairs,' I said, 'while you go and find my mother in the garden. She's dying to meet you.'

My mother liked her straight away and the week-end

11

was spent giving Maria information on how everything worked. I had done this with the 'helps' so often before, it was almost routine. However, I may have shown Maria the deference a man has for a pretty girl, because I remember Mother looking at me sharply once or twice.

In fact, I had not given my mother much cause for jealousy over the years. My regard and love for her were such that I could never bring myself to hurt her seriously. Few women matched up to her in my estimation: strong, intelligent, amusing; facing life with courage and with a great sense of fun. Her arthritic condition was a disaster for a woman of her boundless energy, but she took it philosophically and fussed very little. So, not to upset her, I kept my affairs secret, my girl friends in London. What the eye cannot see . . . Mother never asked me about them.

By my early thirties I had got into somewhat rigid bachelor ways and all my evenings were organized. Monday, I did my chores, and sometimes took home work from the office to go through in the quiet of my flat. I told my girl friends I needed it 'to sort myself out'. Tuesdays was for my love life: girls – or rather the favourite of the moment – I only had one at a time. Wednesday was usually booked for a chess match at my club. Thursday was keep fit evening: tennis in summer, squash in winter. Which brought me to Friday – and back to Mother! I only broke out to go and have dinner every now and again with my partner, Edward, and his wife, Rosemary, whom I adored in a perfectly platonic way.

The girls I met and mated with could never get used to my rigid routine and usually dropped me pretty soon. Marianne, the latest, who had lasted six months, had finally sent a note which did not exactly drip honey. *Sorry, I won't be seeing you any more. Have now found a man*

12

*who likes to sleep with me from Wednesdays to Mondays. So
Tuesdays I'm keeping free to 'sort myself out'.*

I had got used to Marianne and liked her. Pity. Still, I
didn't mind too much. I suppose I was a bit of a cold fish
in those days.

Once, at Mother's, a pretty Australian girl had flirted
with me, and she had been replaced immediately. That is
why I had to tread carefully with Maria.

When I arrived on the following Friday, however, she
was not there.

'Hallo, darling. Why are you alone?' I asked my
mother casually.

'I told Maria she could go out tonight as you would be
coming. She has had no time off yet and I don't want her
to become dissatisfied. She's O.K, streets above the
others, and she doesn't fuss. I can't bear it when they flap
and fuss.'

I breathed freely again. Things were going well.

We would have to get a day off fixed; other than
Friday, though.

So the next morning, while my mother was resting
and I was helping Maria with the washing-up, I said to
her, 'You must fix a regular day off, you know. Mrs
Hoggs is used to standing in. It's good for Mother, and
essential for you, to have a change.'

'I suppose so,' Maria answered, not much interested.
'What day, I wonder.'

'Tuesday,' I said quickly.

'Why Tuesday?'

'Because Mrs Hoggs is free on Tuesdays and Thurs-
days, and I shall be seeing you again on Friday.'

Maria looked at me and smiled, 'Do you come every
week-end?'

'Always. Friday to Sunday night. Sometimes I leave

13

on Monday morning.'

'Quite a tie for you,' she said thoughtfully.

'I have no others,' I answered promptly. 'What about you?'

'Free as air.'

'Good. Will you come up to London next Tuesday, and I'll take you to the theatre, if you like. Let's both live a little. But keep it from Mother. I don't like her to feel left out.'

Her green, luminous eyes looked understandingly into mine. 'You certainly worry over her. You are a very devoted son. All right. Mum's the word.'

And that was the first time we went out together. The following Tuesday we went to a film. She was gay and relaxed, but not in the least flirtatious. When I showed her to her train for home she coolly gave her hand and said, 'Thank you, John. A lovely evening.' And went to her seat. She never waved, blew kisses or did any of the coy things so many women do.

I had known her three weeks before I kissed her on that Saturday. It was in the month of May.

Even here, in Mexico City, in January, after all these months, the thrill of that first contact still moved me. My whisky was finished and I put out the light. I would rather sleep on a happy thought than some of the misery that was to follow. Tomorrow I had promised to go outside Mexico City to an Indian market with my new American friends, and it was getting late.

CHAPTER THREE

We arrived at the Indian market around eleven in the morning. I had apologized for my abrupt departure the night before and they had expressed concern. All was well. The women chattered excitedly in the taxi about the things they intended to buy. Babe pressed herself against me getting in and out.

The Indians were dressed as Indians: head-bands, beads, ponchos – the lot. I had seen so much of this gear in London, it seemed almost familiar. The scene was colourful: the stalls hung about with gay knitwear, leather goods, bright pottery and the usual junk jewellery. On closer inspection, I could see that the average standard of taste was high. Mrs Hoggs had asked for real Indian moccasins, and this seemed my chance to get them. So I said to my American friends, 'I'll leave you and go off on some souvenir hunting. See you at the restaurant in about an hour?'

'Fine,' the wife said. 'I'm just dying to look around too. There sure are some cute things here.'

Babe had already wandered off, exclaiming ecstatically over everything.

Walking past the stalls, I saw many attractive things I would have liked to buy for Maria. But to buy presents for a non-person was madness. I must confine myself to reality and get Mrs Hoggs' moccasins and something for

Rosemary – a piece of jewellery, perhaps. This part of the market was inside a large building and steps led to a gallery which ran all round at a higher level, with yet more stalls on it. I was looking up, considering whether to go and explore that too, when I saw him – the grey man. He was standing on the edge of the gallery, looking down, the pale, cold eyes glinting in my direction, as before.

What was he doing in the Indian market? He hardly looked the type to buy beads, moccasins or bright coloured ponchos. *Was* he dogging my footsteps?

Of course he had a perfect right to be there, along with all the other hundreds of tourists, but I did not like it. Sickened, I turned my back firmly and concentrated on some hand-crafted jewellery on a stall nearby, made by an imposing Indian. I settled for an unusual fob and chain to take back to Rosemary. By the time I turned back and looked up casually, he had gone.

Put off from any further exploration, feeling hot and tense in the crowded market, I hurriedly pushed my way out into the fresh air, and decided to walk to the restaurant to kill time before meeting my friends. I walked briskly, looking over my shoulder every now and then to see if I was being followed.

Why did this man haunt me? He was dark and foreign-looking; he *could* be Greek. He *might* be Maria's father, or someone out to avenge her. But why follow me to Mexico? Why not London? The whole thing was an absolute nonsense, I told myself. An incubus bred from my feverish anxiety and despair. All the same, I was now resolved to leave Mexico City as soon as possible.

The recommended restaurant was a pleasant building in the Spanish tradition: the tables, set under arcades, looked out on to a landscaped garden with a fountain playing in the centre. I sat down in a dark corner and ordered a drink. Mrs Hoggs' moccasins, I realized, had been completely forgotten.

Presently the Americans arrived in a taxi, loaded with parcels and talking, talking. We had reserved a table and made our way to it, I looking round uneasily before settling. Then I sat down with the others.

The sun was bright and the flowers gay in the patio; we ordered more drinks; Babe's chatter flowed over me like a bubbling stream – and I relaxed.

The Swiss chef produced excellent food. I mellowed and began to pay Babe a little attention.

It seemed to go to her head: she talked so fast it was almost incomprehensible. At the end of a long recital of their plans, she added: 'So, John, I sure hope you will join us.'

'I'm afraid I'm leaving for Taxco this afternoon, up in the mountains. My mother would like some hand-crafted Mexican silver. I understand that's where it's made.'

'Oh, no,' she cried, dismayed. 'There is still so much to do in Mexico City. You'll be missing out on it.'

'I aim to return here after a short tour. My Embassy friends will be back and I've promised to visit them before pushing on to Peru.'

It was a half truth. The Embassy 'friends', the Plummers, had never met me. They were Maria's previous employers. It was I who was bent on seeing them. I had been bitterly disappointed on arrival to find that they were away in California on leave. It would fit in very well for me to go now, see something more of Mexico, and return in a few days.

'But – aren't you going to Acapulco?'

'Of course.' I smiled at her anxiety. 'Can't leave out

17

Acapulco. It has magic in its name. I shall probably go there after two or three days in the mountains.'

'Great,' she cried, clapping her hands. 'We'll be there in three days. Where will you be staying?'

I named the hotel booked by my agent in London.

'Why, it's our hotel too. So we *shall* meet again. Promise?'

'Promise,' I said with some warmth. They were a friendly and kindly group and it can be lonely on one's own in a cosmopolitan centre like Acapulco. The prospect of meeting them there again was not displeasing.

Later, having said good-bye to the Americans, I paid the hotel and left my big suitcase behind to await my return. I sank into the hired taxi with a small bag and a sense of escape. From what exactly, was not clear in my mind, but I felt relief as I left Mexico City behind.

It was about a hundred miles to Taxco and I wished I had my Porsche to take me on my way instead of this clattering old taxi. Fast cars fascinate me and driving them is a form of release from my tensions. Now, bored with gazing at prickly cactus and aloes and huge agaves in the arid countryside through which we were passing, I closed my eyes and let my mind drift back to the Grand Prix of last year – that fabulous week-end which, at last, decisively changed my relationship with Maria . . .

After I had kissed Maria on that Saturday, she seemed to avoid me. Determined to stop this nonsense, I tackled her over the washing-up next day.

'Maria, you're not really angry with me, for heaven's sake. It was only a harmless kiss. What shall we do on Tuesday?'

'I'm not angry, of course, John. Just cautious. I don't

18

want to be hurt again. Let's not see each other on Tuesdays for a bit.'

'Not see each other? What absolute rubbish! Why are you so cautious? Are you afraid I shall rape you or something? What *is* all this about?'

'John, dear, rape is probably not as painful as rejected love. I've been through all that – and it hurt like hell. There was a boy in Athens, at University. He was in his last year, I in my second. We became lovers. My first and only affair: Nikos – that was his name. I thought that we were going to get married as soon as he had got his degree and a job. One day, towards the end of his final year, he came to me and told me quite calmly that his parents wanted him to marry a girl they had chosen for him, who had a rich dowry. She was willing and, it seems, so was he. It would set him up in practice, he said. He was to be a dental surgeon and the equipment was expensive. This sort of arranged marriage is still quite usual in Greece.'

She had stopped washing-up; the mop idle in her hand she stared out of the window into the distance.

'So?' I asked, to bring her back.

'So – at first I just couldn't believe it. All that passion, love, fun we had shared – how could he so lightly dismiss it? He had meant everything to me.' She resumed the washing-up. 'I won't bore you with details. My pride made me put on a silly brave face, and he admired, he said, my spirit! Shortly after, his engagement was announced, and he went to America for a year to complete his training. I never saw him again.'

'And you?' I asked gently.

'Me? I gave up University. I couldn't concentrate. Through an introduction, I took on the job with the Plummers at the Embassy. They were going back to England, and I wanted to get away. I enjoyed being with

19

them. They treated me as family and the kids were sweet. When they had to move on, I decided to stay on in England because I had regained my composure and a certain peace of mind in this friendly country. So here I am. Still licking my wounds a little – but they are healing. I don't want to start all that up again. I want to stay at peace.'

There was a silence between us when she finished. I was polishing a glass over and over. Never has a glass received such a brilliant shine. My reactions were an uneasy mixture of guilt and pity. I thought of the girls who had shed tears over me; I decided to be as honest as possible with Maria.

'Look, Maria, you had a rotten deal and, as you say, the scars are still with you; but they will heal. That's life: one learns to take the knocks. Look at my mother. She loses her husband in the war and has to bring me up on her own. She didn't re-marry, she once told me, because she loved me too much and feared any new husband might be jealous. Then, this wretched condition she has – the pain, and worse, the enforced inactivity. Well, in a way I suppose, it's blighted my own life a little though I don't look at it like that. I love my mother and stay single so that I may devote most of my spare time to her. It wouldn't be fair to any wife to take me on on those conditions – also my mother would feel rejected and it just wouldn't be fair on her either. So I don't get married. So I have affairs – naturally. Well, usually the girls get fed up and chuck me.' I shrugged. 'I suppose some may think it caddish, but my reasons are those, that's how it is. I'm not the type to force myself on anyone but I do enjoy going out with you and if you enjoy it too, for goodness sake let's continue. No strings. That I promise. Is it on?'

We looked at each other. I expect my obvious anxiety

20

to placate and convince her melted her resolution. She burst out laughing.

'You are so earnest, John. I don't agree altogether with everything you say, but I get your point. I enjoy going out with you too, you see, and I would miss it. So, all right, it's on. Where are we going?'

That Tuesday we went to a concert. Every week we did something different and I began to live for the simple excitement of meeting Maria and just being with her. We were more relaxed with each other since our talk. Telling me about her unhappiness seemed to have released her inner broodings a little and perhaps the image of the loved one was receding. She laughed a lot and teased me, though never flirtatiously. I was gentle with her; she needed understanding and I know she appreciated it.

Of course, however good my intentions, this situation could not remain static. I wanted her more every time I saw her. I longed restlessly for an opportunity to present itself, to break down the barrier of her subconscious resistance, to make her come willingly to me without pressure.

It was nearly June and one of my richer clients, knowing my passion for fast cars and anxious to show his gratitude for the help I had given him, invited me to go down to his apartment in Monte Carlo for the week-end of the Grand Prix.

For once, I was feverishly anxious to get away. I tackled my mother immediately on the week-end preceding it.

'Look, Mother darling,' I said, coming straight to the point. 'Mr and Mrs Rogers have asked me to go and stay with them for the Grand Prix in Monte Carlo next Sunday. I'd like to go if you will stay with Kate Hetherington.'

21

Lady Hetherington was one of my mother's oldest friends, who still lived in some style. She was always pressing Mother to go and stay a few days for a change but it was nearly two years since Mother had been last.

'You go, Johnny,' Mother said. 'I don't need to leave here. I shall be all right with Maria.'

But I was very firm, for me.

'No, darling. You need a change. It will be good for you. This is a splendid opportunity, and Maria should have a break, too,' I added boldly. Of course, I was quite determined to get her to come with me.

My mother argued and grumbled a bit, but I made the point that I would enjoy myself more knowing she was in good hands, and finally she capitulated. I was immediately on the phone to Lady Hetherington, who appeared delighted to have Mother. We arranged that I should drive her down on Friday evening and Lady H would return Mother on Monday. Now it only remained for me to convince Maria.

That Friday at dinner, we talked quite openly about our plans for the next week-end.

My mother said to Maria, 'And what will you do with your free week-end? Where will you go?'

Maria thought for a second. 'I think I'd like to swim. Yes. That's what I'll do. Swim and swim. That's if this lovely weather holds. I may go to a place near Brighton where I stayed with the Plummer children sometimes. The woman who runs the small hotel knows me.'

She spoke, of course, with absolute conviction and innocence, so that even if my mother had entertained any doubts they must have been instantly dispelled.

I did not get a chance to speak to Maria privately that evening and spent most of the night awake, thinking up ways of convincing her to come away with me.

I need not have worried. On Saturday, when the golden hour of washing-up together arrived, in spite of all
my careful thinking, I blurted out directly, 'Maria, how
would you like to come with me to Monte Carlo and
swim in the warm Mediterranean instead of that cold,
grey Channel?'

Her eyes widened and her mouth dropped open
slightly in surprise. 'John, what a marvellous idea!' she
said.

Then we made plans . . .

The Mexican taxi driver said something to me and I
pushed down my thoughts and opened my eyes. The
driver was pointing to two children by the dusty road,
holding up what looked like a small dragon by a string
tied to its tail.

'Iguana,' the driver was saying. 'Very good eat. You
want?'

He slowed down and the children became excited and
waved the creature up and down, making tracks for the
taxi, inciting me to buy.

I looked at this huge lizard hanging upside down, alive
and wriggling desperately. Poor thing! I had a good mind
to buy it and set it free. But it would probably only be
caught again and sold to a less soft-hearted customer.

'No, no. Drive on,' I said quickly, upset by the sight.
Strange that I could be so soft-hearted over some things
and so callous over others.

I stopped thinking about Maria and gave my mind to
the surroundings. The giant cactus, the dry mountainous
landscape, had a certain harsh excitement. Here and there
a farmhouse stood, lonely in the desolate countryside. I
wondered how anyone made a living in such arid land.

We climbed higher into the mountains, softened by the twilight, deep in shadows. Eventually, the sparkling lights of Taxco burst into my vision round a bend, for by now it was night and I could see nothing of the town except its lights.

The taxi drew up at a hotel on the outskirts. I stepped thankfully into the courtyard and took a deep breath. The air smelt good and was refreshingly cool. I sighed with pleasure. Peace at last . . .

CHAPTER FOUR

A strange tinkling sound wove through my dreams in the morning. It was rhythmic and continuous. A million clocks, with silver chimes, gone beserk and all striking at once. I opened my eyes and through my open window saw Taxco spread out on the mountains. It was familiar – like an oil painting seen many times before. White-washed houses with rosy tiles; Bougainvillæa and geraniums streaming down the walls. In the middle distance, a baroque church of perfect proportions, giving balance and point to the composition.

Where was I? Back in the Mediterranean with Maria? For a moment I was bewildered. My eyes, accustomed to the wastelands of yesterday, were stunned at the sight of so much colour and harmony again.

As my mind cleared, I realized that this, being the centre of the tin and silver mines exploited by the Spaniards over many years, a prosperous and beautiful town had grown out of their wealth and taste.

I was to learn that the tinkling sound, which was a part of the scene, came from the eight hundred workshops. It was the symphony of a million small hammers beating on silver, fashioning chains, jewellery, masks, and ornaments of every kind.

I liked this place. When I had breakfasted I would explore it quietly.

The hotel was pink and spacious; built, Spanish-style, in a quadrangle around green gardens and a blue swimming pool. In the end, I was loath to leave its peace and comfort. Time enough to explore tomorrow. Just now, the rising sun was hot and the pool cool.

In and out of the water, stretched on a deck chair, I felt relaxed – for the first time since that terrible day with Maria. Was this what I wanted? Had I come to Mexico seeking the Plummers, or peace of mind?

My new thriller lay on my knees, but my eyes had drifted to the blue water of the pool, and I saw Maria again as she came out of the sea, dripping and gleaming, and lay beside me on the raft, rocking gently on the smooth Mediterranean. It was so covered in gull droppings, we were hard put to it to find a clean spot.

She was a wonderful swimmer, but I was stronger than she and had beat her to the raft. She stretched out beside me and I turned over to look at her. She was beautiful in her bikini. I had never seen her so naked before. The sun had brought out a few faint freckles and she was glowing with the swim. Her black hair streamed long and wet on her shoulders. I wanted to lick the drops off her face; my eyes were fixed on her mouth.

'You look good enough to eat,' I said, crowding up on her.

'Stop it, John. I'm enjoying myself. Don't spoil it.'

I stopped myself from kissing her. 'Well, if you won't let me eat you, let's get back for some real food. I'm hungry after the cotton wool and plastic on the plane. Come on.' And laughing, we pushed each other into the water. This time I let her win the race back.

We had arrived in Nice that Saturday around two

26

o'clock in the afternoon. Maria looked rapturous as we stepped off the plane when she saw the blue sea and waving palms and felt the hot sun beating off the tarmac. She took big sniffs of air and said, 'Let's go and swim at once.'

'When we've driven to our hotel and checked in – it's near Monte Carlo and about an hour's drive away,' I said, pleased at her pleasure. 'Then, I promise, we'll go. I could do with a swim, too.'

We got into the hired car and I drove along the Moyenne Corniche to a little hotel up one of the valleys, on the far side of Monte Carlo. I know the Côte well. My mother and I spent many holidays there before she became inactive.

My friends, the Rogers, had accepted without comment that I should be bringing a girl friend to their party on the day of the Grand Prix, but that I would not be staying. They could think what they liked. Though I doubt whether they, in fact, gave it another thought.

The car race was not until Sunday. Meanwhile I had Maria to myself for the rest of Saturday.

After our swim, we went back to our hotel for a shower and change. Maria, of course, insisted on having her own room – also that she should pay for it. I did not argue. She wanted it that way; and it was not an expensive hotel.

We drove into the mountains for dinner. I knew of this unpretentious restaurant, run by a family, where the food was always freshly cooked and good. At least, I hoped it would be there unchanged; it was some years since I had been.

The family were still running it and remembered me. There were many exclamations and questions to be posed and answered before we could settle to the business of eating.

'How's your mother?'

'Well, not so mobile these days, but she's cheerful.'

Monsieur le patron wore a beret and had a twinkle in his eye. He looked in admiration at Maria. *'Toujours avec les jolies femmes,'* he said.

Maria laughed gaily. I could have wagered my all that she had not thought of her University student once that day.

We ate fresh trout cooked in herbs over a wood fire; potatoes in their jackets, followed by ravioli prepared by Mamma with her own special savoury filling. A green salad, strawberries, a runny Brie and quantities of the Rosé wine of the region. We finished with strong black coffee and a local 'marc' – heady stuff that took the enamel off your teeth and made you feel you owned the world.

The sun, sinking behind the mountains, bathed everything in a particularly rosy glow. Far away, down the V of the valley, the sea was visible, a few white-sailed boats glinting on it as they caught the last rays of light.

Maria sighed contentedly. 'Perfect,' she said.

I covered her hand with mine. 'Only because you're here.'

'John,' she pleaded. But I kept my hand on hers and looked at her steadily. I wanted her with every nerve in my body. I wanted to be in our hotel.

We drove back slowly at her request. She had never been to this part of the world before and although it reminded her of Greece, she said, it was different: lusher, greener, though not necessarily more beautiful.

Walking through the hotel gardens, by now in darkness, a firefly darted out in front of us, pulsing and glowing away with tremendous energy. I caught it in my

28

hand and it went on lighting the inside of my palm in little flashes. Maria was enthralled. 'But let it go,' she said 'It can't enjoy being captive.' She felt as I did about such things.

Early June is, I believe, my favourite month for the south of France. Warm without being too hot; the vegetation not yet dried up. Flowers and birds abound. As we went upstairs to our bedrooms, we heard it – the nightingale. Anyone who has not heard a nightingale must be bored stiff with descriptions of its song. But if you *do* hear it, there is no dismissing its magic.

Maria ran up the stairs to the open window on the landing just outside our rooms. She stood there entranced and I stood with her, listening to the repeated trills of the bird as it went through the gamut of its emotions. I've read that this is not intended as a love song; it is merely a triumphant proclamation of the owner's territorial rights. That may be; nevertheless, love is the emotion it arouses. I put my arm round Maria and kissed her gently on the mouth. She resisted at first, but not too fiercely. I kissed her again, more passionately and she was trembling now. It was delicious, and in a kind of delirium, I caught her in my arms, kicked open my bedroom door and carried her on to the bed.

Our need must have been mutual for we came together in a wild fusion. Her passion was like a flame, consuming me, though she was not at all clever about sex. I was glad. I prefer to be the leader, the possessor. When women try to take over, it seems to destroy something in me – the flowering of tenderness, perhaps. In spite of her previous lover, there was about Maria a sweet innocence, a ravishing surrender to my masculinity, that made me fall instantly and deeply in love with her.

I closed my eyes now and let the happiness of that first night flow over me.

A harsh voice crashed through my thoughts: 'Over here, girls. Here's the pool. Ain't that just darling?'

The 'girls' were a group of women ranging in years from fifty to eighty, judging by their looks. They quickly monopolized all the chairs and some went into cabins and came out in cute, girly swim wear. Raucous voices filled the air. Shapeless bodies plunged into the pool.

It was too much. I took myself off to the refuge of the bar and thence to an early lunch. The restaurant was packed out. Touring the South Americas, I decided, was all right provided you could stand the other tourists.

Fortunately these groups were only there for a few hours. They lunched, and by 3.30 they all left, and peace was restored.

I decided to spend the rest of the afternoon writing to my mother. It calmed me to think of her.

My mother had looked years younger and more cheerful than I had seen her in months, when she came back from that week-end with Lady H. Kate Hetherington was a big woman. Her husband had died leaving her a pile of money and everything about her was big: her house, her garden, her activities. She was bursting with energy and good works. Nothing was too much trouble. Her heart was the biggest thing about her.

'Of course, Kate is quite dotty,' my mother was saying, when we sat down to supper on the Monday of our return. Maria and I had caught a morning plane from Nice and were there in good time to welcome her.

'Do you know what she did?' Mother continued. 'She

took me along to this fête where it was intended that she should present the prizes and announced that I was going to do it instead. She spoke of me as though I were some sort of a heroine of the last war. You would think I had been parachuted into France and tortured by the Gestapo, the way she talked about my courage and endurance. Such nonsense. Hallo,' she greeted Maria, who had just come in with some food. 'You're looking very happy. I forgot to ask whether you went to the sea?'

'Yes,' Maria said. 'I had a wonderful time.'

'You've certainly caught the sun,' said Mother, and then went straight on with her recital. 'So there I was on the platform in my wheel chair, presenting prizes, and people came and shook my hand with great respect – some even kissed it. I thought they would kiss my feet next.' My mother had obviously enjoyed herself enormously. Kate Hetherington was truly fond of her and had made sure Mother would get all the distraction and morale boosting she could give her. Wonderful woman.

It meant also that Mother was so full of her own excitements she did not enquire too closely into ours.

I finished my letter to her and went to bed. That night I had my recurring dream about Maria. She was swimming and I was trying to catch up with her, but in vain. The blue sea turned black and a huge wave rose ahead of me. I always woke before it engulfed me. I was sweating with terror.

After an uneasy night, I was thankful to be wakened again in the morning by the myriad tinkling of the silver workers. Today I would go out and explore the shops and town in search of something beautiful for my mother. Skulking in the hotel was not good enough.

After breakfast I bravely ventured out into the heat.

Taxco was even more attractive on close inspection than from a distance. The houses were in pink, white, and pale blue washes. Spanish tiles in bold colours, depicting holy scenes, were on some of the outside walls. There were niches for saints, wrought-iron staircases, and grills. Brilliant flowers cascaded down the walls. The streets, being on different levels up the sides of the mountains, were connected by winding steps. It had the charm of so many Mediterranean small towns that I wandered about happily, feeling at home.

Busy workers in the factories and shops were tapping away at their craft. The owners showed me with pride some of their more valued possessions, and I chose for my mother a linked chain which had won a prize. Passing a window displaying several masks, I noticed one made in silver, with a madonna-like face and milky green, semi-precious stones for eyes. It was beautiful and reminded me of Maria. Without counting the cost I went in and bought it.

On the way out I stopped, riveted by a silver mesh necklace inset with citrines. It would have looked lovely on Maria's sunburnt skin and the stones were made to match her eyes. Compulsively, I bought that too. Bad thinking – and expensive. Still, I told myself, it could become a part of my collection.

I am a dilettante collector. Not specializing in anything, just buying what pleases me. Having no family, I have little else on which to spend my considerable income. My mother is well able to look after herself financially.

My flat in London is crammed with innumerable exciting things – exciting to me, anyway. My tastes are catholic. A Henry Moore statuette stands on a Queen

32

Anne cabinet, and the Etruscan head I picked up as a bargain looks superb on a plain perspex table lit up from below.

Convinced that all elegant things blend regardless of age or geography, this mixture of ancient and modern delights me; a Picasso pot which I placed beside a three-thousand-year-old Greek one, at first glance could have been fashioned by the same hand.

Amongst the motley collection on my walls are a few rare icons from Byzantium, and these especially pleased Maria. She would spend a great deal of time looking at my treasures with me. We both loved beautiful things and I loved her – beautiful above everything I possessed. But she, my special treasure, was now lost to me. How could I have done what I did to her? How could I?

I had reached the main Plaza on which stood the small baroque Borda Cathedral. It was exquisite. I went into its coolness and quiet and sat down.

The Spaniards, who had felt the spiritual drive to create the Cathedral as an expression of their love of God had, on the other hand, perpetrated untold cruelties in His name in this same country. That there is no excuse for cruelty I knew only too well. This dichotomy is in us all, I mused: undisciplined, the evil side could ultimately take over. I rose wearily – the church had not soothed me; it had made me feel even more unworthy.

Opposite the Cathedral was a café and I sat down to have an iced beer. The pleasant square, sunny and colourful, should have cheered me: why then did I feel uneasy? I looked round, and just coming out of the Cathedral, was the grey man.

He stood a moment, with that quality of stillness that was his, and the pale eyes turned towards me. He must have been in the dark Cathedral while I had been sitting

33

there. The hair on the back of my neck literally rose like a cat's at the thought. I was cold and sweaty all over suddenly. I could not bear his look and turned my chair round with my back to him. Finishing my beer quickly, I went into the interior of the café to pay, fearing he would walk over. But when I came out again, he had vanished. Had he gone back into the Cathedral?

There were taxis lined up in the square, and I hurried into the first one and asked to be driven to my hotel.

The relative peace I had found in Taxco was shattered. At my request, the hotel porter booked me on the bus that was leaving for Acapulco that afternoon.

CHAPTER FIVE

It was night again when I arrived in Acapulco. Lights glittered everywhere. The hotel lobby was bulging with visitors clamouring for their rooms. For a dreadful moment it looked as though the hotel would be unable to accommodate me as they had not been expecting me till tomorrow. I was thankful when the desk clerk said, 'O.K.'

Did I want to go on any of the organized tours that night? he asked me. No, I was tired, I said: my friends were arriving the next day and time enough to go on tours with them. Could I have a steak and a bottle of whisky sent up to me tonight, please?

I went to my room and looked out of the window. We were not far from the edge of the sea and I could hear the waves beating on the shore and see the white flash of the breakers. The hotel was on the end of a large bay, curving in a horseshoe and studded with lights, so that they shone across the waters ahead of me. It looked a big place and the noise of the coaches as they drove off with load after load of tourists to see the sights, indicated that it was also very popular.

I looked forward to the arrival of my American friends. Babe and her brother and his wife now represented to me a comforting normality, a cushion against my morbid fears and anxieties. I would be happy to have their companionship again and left a note to greet them on their arrival. Meanwhile, a bottle of whisky would keep me company this evening.

The waiter arrived with the meal I had ordered and I fell upon it ravenously, then I got up and locked the door, feeling a little ridiculous over my fears. Pouring a stiff whisky, I unpacked in a leisurely manner, gloating over my new treasures.

The silver mask I hung on a hook on the wall. It gazed down on me sorrowfully. I stared for a long time at the mesh necklace and wondered how it would have suited Maria. I had never given her any jewellery. She was not demanding and looked quite lovely unadorned, so that it had not occurred to me. Only once she had said, 'I would like to keep this as a reminder of our happiness right now,' and taken a plain gold scarf ring that I wore with my silk cravat at the time.

It had been on that same fabulous week-end of the Grand Prix . . .

Everything about it had had a magic touch. On the Sunday the weather was perfect, even for Monte Carlo.

We stood on the balcony in the sunlight, watching the cars roaring round. The Rogers' flat was about ten floors up and strategically well placed for a view of the race: just above the start line, so that we always knew who was leading on each new lap. After a while, we could not stand the continual assault on our ear drums and went into the comparative quiet of the room. Pink champagne was being passed round. We moved about to mix with the other people. I heard Maria say, 'No, I'm not Mrs Devigne. Just a guest here.'

Mrs Devigne, I thought, and a pleased thrill went

through me, instantly suppressed. My mother would never agree. Marriage would be too difficult and cause endless problems.

'What a lucky break,' the man was answering Maria. 'Whenever I come to Monte, I live in the hope of finding a dishy girl like you to take around and have a bit of fun with. Usually the good lookers are all married.' He was sunburnt, with dark curly hair, and thought himself one hell of a guy; he was also a little drunk.

'Surely Soho would be an easier hunting ground for bits of fun,' murmured Maria's cool voice.

That's shaken his routine, I thought with satisfaction.

That morning, Maria had insisted that we get up early to have a swim before going to the party. It was so wonderful to be able at last to stroke her hair and skin and kiss her mouth, without all that 'don't touch me' stuff, that I would have been happy just to stay in our room alone with her all day. However, of course, I gave in.

We had our swim, showered and dressed. Maria needed no make-up. She had caught the sun and glowed all over. She wore a sea-green silky dress and had piled her black hair on top, with wisps curling and falling about her face. She looked stunning.

As we were not expected before one o'clock, we had plenty of time to wander about the crowded streets of Monte Carlo, hand in hand, then to sit awhile with cooling drinks in the square, watching the thousands of people milling around. There was an atmosphere of holiday and excitement, and the roar of the cars revving and having test runs was a constant background.

Maria said, 'Oh, to go through life just sitting in the sun, watching car races and drinking iced lemonade!'

I made a face. 'I would need something a bit stronger to drink. Otherwise I might well die of non-alcoholic poisoning.'

I kissed the inside of her hand. She stroked my face. We were utterly relaxed.

The route the cars were to take was barricaded off, and the main spectator stands were alongside it. Hundreds of people, however, had taken up their positions already in all the available free space; tight-packed masses were sitting up the sides of the hill leading to the romantic Monagasque Palace: others were on small boats lazing in the harbour. Looking down on the crowds from our high balcony later, they seemed, in their multi-coloured clothes, like bright dots of Hundreds and Thousands stuck on a birthday cake. The sea was incredibly blue.

There were nearly forty laps to go still when we went on the balcony again after lover-boy had made his pass at Maria. It was a very exciting car race. The leading car was red, and driven by an Englishman. Lap after lap he led the way. About third place was held by the current favourite – non-English. It was a black car, long and lean, and the way it easily kept in third place was rather sinister.

Every ten laps or so Maria and I went back into the room for another glass of pink champagne and to rest our battered ears. The hours were passing swiftly. Casanova cast several lecherous glances in Maria's direction, but I wasn't standing for it, and stayed firmly beside her.

Whenever we went back on to the balcony, the red English car was still roaring by in first place and Maria clapped with glee. Suddenly, about three laps from the end, the sinister black number three, zoomed into second place. The leap in tension was tremendous; Maria grasped my arm urgently; her thick-skinned admirer came and leant beside her, using the lack of space as an excuse to squeeze too near. However, there was no time to think of anything but the race now.

When next the red car appeared round a bend, the wolfish black was gaining on it. Any minute, one felt, it would be overwhelmed. But red still tore bravely past and round again. One lap before the end it was touch and go. Maria was making gasping sounds of terror, completely absorbed. When red appeared again, black was almost nose to tail. They roared down the hill – by the sea front – and as they were going round the final bend, the over eager black hit one of the bumpers, just a touch, but enough to throw him off balance for a precious second, and English red came triumphantly into the straight and was flagged down – the winner.

Maria jumped up and down. 'We've won, England's won,' she cried as the Union Jack was run up and the National Anthem played. She was so overcome she was almost in tears. I put my arm around her and hugged her and led her into the room, ignoring curly Casanova's attempts at conversation.

We stayed to have a few words with our hosts, but it was getting late and time to make our good-byes. It took some while to extricate ourselves from the long traffic hold-ups; then we were suddenly in the clear and soon arrived at the restaurant to which I was taking Maria that night.

'Wonderful race, wonderful party,' Maria was saying as we settled down at our table.

'Yes, except for that creep who kept chasing you.'

'Darling,' she said, taking my hand, 'it was the most pathetic waste of effort.'

I held her hand tight and caught her knees between mine under the table. We looked at each other, fixedly. She gave a faint smile. I knew, like me, that she did not want to waste too much precious time over dinner.

That night, it was even better than the previous one.

She was less inhibited; tenderness and passion grew between us. I had never been so happy before. If outside the nightingale was again singing its possessive song, it was for others. I had Maria, a bed, and the soothing darkness of the room, binding us closer in intimacy, covering us with its velvety quiet.

I must have fallen asleep at last. When I awoke, daylight was streaming through the shutters, and Maria was sitting up, gazing down on me. Her black hair hung in a curtain on each side of her pale face. 'You know I love you, Johnnie,' she said, and kissed me tremulously on the mouth.

'I'm crazy about you too, Maria,' I said. 'Just crazy about you.' It was the best I could do – a compromise. The long habit of self-discipline in such matters prevented me from admitting that I was deeply in love with her.

I pulled her down on top of me and held her there; her flesh felt warm and her heart beat against mine. I looked at my wrist watch. It was only 7 a.m. Though we had to catch a plane later that morning, there was still time.

She moaned sweetly at first when I made love to her. Clinging to me desperately, wildly, she abandoned herself to her passion, crying out her love.

When it was over, she lay quietly, a tear slowly trickling into her hair line. 'John, my darling,' she whispered, 'it's never been like this before. It was wonderful.'

'Wonderful,' I repeated, licking away her tear, kissing her tenderly, possessively, all over. She tasted salty with sweat. My own was pouring off my body, mingling with hers. We lay there soaked, exhausted, content.

Her words had flooded my mind with happiness. I felt the same. There was that special spark between us, which some may call divine, in that it only ignites between two chosen people. Our passion was not spent with the act of love; out of it flowed a stream of tenderness and joy and peace beyond anything I had imagined or experienced before.

I think, given the opportunity, I would have married Maria that week-end. The opportunity did not arise and the golden moment passed. Selfishly reluctant to disturb my easy life, we simply returned to London and slipped back into the routine of looking after Mother and sharing our Tuesdays together.

Mother, of course, was the excuse with which I bludgeoned my mind into this insensitive complacency. She relied on me, I kept telling myself, and I must not upset her in any way.

It was she, however, who was the innocent instigator in providing Maria and me with the chance to go away on our own once more: that week-end later in the summer, which had led to the final disaster.

I could not bear to go on thinking about it now.

Maudlin and fanciful with half a bottle of whisky inside me, I saw a tear on the sad face of the silver mask. Rousing myself from the depths of my armchair, I went close – to find, of course, that it was only a shadow. I bent to kiss the mouth with longing; but the lips felt cold and dead.

CHAPTER SIX

Babe greeted me ecstatically when she saw me in the lobby next morning. 'Look who's here, sugar,' she cried to her sister-in-law. 'If it isn't our Johnnie. You don't look good,' she said as she embraced me. 'Are you all right, honey?'

'I'm O.K. Just a bit hung up. I've been lonely. It's good to see you again.' In some twisted way I meant it.

'Sugar' came over and greeted me. 'Jack's gone to get tickets to see the sights tonight. We'd sure love you to come with us,' she said

'O.K. I'll go and find him at the booking office.'

Jack gave me a warm welcome too. The Americans' social manner of making you feel loved, even if it is a lot of 'bull', can be very comforting. I let myself fall under its spell and went along soporifically with my little group.

We bought tickets for the perilous divers that night. Meanwhile, Babe took me over on our return from the ticket office. 'It's so damn hot, we're going to have a swim. Why not come and join us, John?'

So I did.

The beach was packed with holiday-makers. Row upon row of deck chairs. Indian hawkers wound their way through them, continually selling their wares: pottery, ponchos, beads – all the usual things. They were a nuisance but, after all, they had to make a living; poverty amongst them was rife.

We were in and out of the water in the great heat. Eager young boys sold us iced Coca-cola and beer. The oval bay was surrounded by mountains, the slopes coming right down into the blue waters of the Pacific. Fliers on kites, pulled above the sea by fast motor-boats, were a source of constant wonder. Flying through the air in their black skin suits, they looked like witches going to a tryst. Had Maria been with me, no doubt we would have attempted a turn at this fascinating stunt. We were both adept at sporty things. Life could have been so much fun with her. How I longed to be back on our raft with its gull droppings and Maria beside me . . .

I thought back over last summer: it had been idyllic. Maria accepted our Tuesdays together as being enough. It was her day off; she had no other. For me, of course, it was the routine of almost a lifetime. The only difference being that I was in love with Maria.

On fine days I sometimes took the afternoon off and we went on the river. We would take a punt and find a good spot to swim. Maria enjoyed swimming. On rainy Tuesdays, either she or I would cook a meal and we just stayed in the flat and made love. We never let the day pass without going back to the flat at some point.

I was happy and everyone remarked on how well I looked. At dinner one night with my partner and his wife, Rosemary, she said, quizzing me: 'John, I've never seen you look better. You must be in love.' I laughed it off, of course. They were a dear family, they and their three children, Jane, Helena and baby John – named after me, his godfather. I should have told them about Maria, shouted my love to the house tops, but instead I had this morbid fear of discovery and sat on it like a guilty secret.

Maria had grown, if possible, more beautiful. Her luminous eyes seemed enormous in her lovely face. When she came into a room, she brought a radiance with her, and my heart would tighten with longing.

About two months had passed since our week-end in Monte Carlo. It was nearing September and my mother was embroidering in the garden while I punished the weeds, when she suddenly announced, 'That dotty Kate's been on the phone again. What do you think she wants me to do now? She's giving a big charity fête in aid of Thalidomide children and is holding it in her garden. She's asked me to dress up as a gypsy and tell fortunes. Of course, she knows I was quite a student of palmistry in the old days, so it's not as crazy as it sounds.'

'How absolutely splendid, darling,' I said, and gave up weeding to sit beside her and discuss it.

'I could wear that mantilla you bought me in Spain and my gold ear-rings,' Mother went on, her eyes bright. 'Kate said she would have a special tent erected with "Come and hear the gypsy's warning – 10p only" written on it. I will be sitting inside and could disguise the wheel chair with one of those jolly Toledo blankets.' Mother went on like this for some time while my mind was busy planning my own week-end – or rather, my own and Maria's.

'And what will *you* do?' she finished.

'I shall go fishing in Devon,' I said promptly.

'And Maria will go swimming again, I suppose?' Did I detect a dry note? Though we were careful to act casually in front of Mother, our urgent need to be together may have unavoidably shown through.

I shrugged, as though it were no concern of mine.

'Probably. Would you like that crystal ball thing I have

44

in London as a prop?' I asked to distract her.

'That seems a good idea,' she said. 'Of course, telling fortunes from a crystal ball is all nonsense, though it impresses people. But the hand does give a very definite indication of character, and as character is mostly destiny, it is not difficult to arrive at some fairly accurate conclusions and give the clients fair value for their money.' She was already completely absorbed in her coming role.

I dragged myself back to the present, hearing Babe say, 'Shall we go and lunch on the terrace? I'm hungry.'

Jack was reading a newspaper. I could not have been a very amusing companion as I was silent, dreaming about the past most of the time.

However, I made an effort and chatted to Babe through the meal. Afterwards we all went to our rooms for a siesta. I thought Babe looked at me meaningfully, and with very little encouragement, I believe she would have joined me. But I simply did not feel up to it. My mind was burdened with anxiety and frustration most of the time. I just threw myself on to my bed and gazed at the silver mask on the wall. Its cool, sad look was not really like Maria, who had an outgoing, sparkling personality. I remembered how I had been burning to discuss my plans with her on the Tuesday following the conversation with my mother . . .

I had prepared a chicken casserole for that evening. Maria had gone to the August sales and I knew she would be tired.

I enjoy cooking. It comforts me: just the feel of onions

or tomatoes in my hand, as I slice and peel, salting the meat, watching the juices run together, gives me real pleasure. I had started when my mother first became weary with illness, and soon grew expert under her guidance. But later, I evolved my own dishes and took a pride in them.

When I first cooked a meal for Maria, she had joked. 'No wonder you've never married. You're such an excellent cook, you don't need a wife.'

She never made remarks like that after we became lovers. She never pressed me to say that I loved her. She was quite exceptional in her control and tact. Perhaps she did not want to upset the delicate balance of our relationship by making me feel uncomfortable in any way.

Presently she came in, dropped her shopping on a chair and kissed me. 'Your mother's been in a frenzy of activity reading up her books on palmistry,' she laughed. 'She insisted on practising on me – my hands are quite worn out. She's most concerned because, she claims, it is painfully obvious that my heart strongly rules my head.'

'Your romantic notions will get you into trouble,' I teased, and kissed her again. 'Now come and have a drink. I want to talk to you about our trip to Devon.'

Maria looked strangely disturbed when I had finished. 'I wonder if we should, Johnnie?' She frowned. 'Maybe it's absurd, but I feel somehow that we are being deceitful to your mother.'

Her thinking had always been straight. The mean twist was in me.

Guilt-ridden, I shut my eyes on the mask now, in effect trying to blot out my own image. Turning over on the bed, I fell asleep. When I awoke, refreshed, it was quite late. I had a leisurely bath and dressed. Later that evening

46

I was due to dine with my American friends and savour the thrills of the perilous divers.

CHAPTER SEVEN

While sitting at our dinner table, anticipating the event of the divers, a new thought came to me about the grey man.

Had he been a relative of Maria's, surely he would have tackled me by now? No, he must be a detective sent to track me down, seeking to catch me out in some way. If one's daughter disappears off the face of the earth, would not her parents be taking some action to find out the cause? Perhaps they had written to my mother and she had answered that she knew nothing. By tacit agreement, we never discussed Maria now. In her letters home, Maria may have unconsciously revealed something of our relationship to her parents, so they had decided to set someone secretly on my trail. Well, I seemed to have thrown him off the scent. On the other hand it was a possibility that, like me, he had also come to Mexico to sound out Maria's previous employers, the Plummers. But the Plummers had not been there. They were due back, the secretary had informed me, in about five days. That was nearly a week ago. Another day in Acapulco was the most I would spend, then back to Mexico City to seek them out. I was not quite sure what I would say. In a way I dreaded drawing attention to myself, yet I felt compelled to follow up my original intention in coming out here. So ran my feverish thoughts. Babe's voice cut in excitedly: 'Here they come – the divers.'

I looked round. The hotel terraces had filled up with coach loads of tourists, arrived to see this spectacle. Making their way across a lower terrace towards their cliff top positions, were the three intrepid men who were about to plunge from a great height into a narrow canyon where the sea swirled black and frightening. The leader stopped, turned towards us and bowed to the applause. As he straightened up, his eyes seemed to glitter in my direction. I leapt to my feet, a cry choked out of me. The leader, I could have sworn, was the grey man. He had the same lean, grim look, and his clothes and appearance were grey.

'What is it, John?' Babe jumped up too and looked to see what had alarmed me.

'Heavens,' I said, 'that man, the leader, he's the – he's just like a man I know,' I ended lamely.

'That's Sanchos, the father. The others are his sons. You've surely made a mistake, John.'

'Of course I have. It's a nonsense. Sorry.' I sat down, feeling an hysterical fool.

'My, but you are jumpy,' said the sister-in-law. 'You look as though you've seen a ghost.'

'Let's all have another drink,' Jack said soothingly.

I knocked back a whisky. If I didn't watch my nerves. I would soon be in a strait jacket.

The three men took up their positions spaced round the cliffs. Flaring torches lit up their actions in the dark night.

The considerable crowds that had gathered to watch them were hushed. Then a great shout went up as the first, my supposed grey man, plunged 130 feet to the foaming sea below.

Torches lit up the narrow black strip of water and we could see him swim to safety. Then the second and the third hurled themselves in. It was soon over. A piece of grit in the eye and one would have missed the whole thing. The crowds were clapping uproariously. Was it for the sound of this sweet music, I wondered, that these men risked death every night?

I had often queried this in my mind when watching acrobats, or people who jumped through flames, or anyone who took spectacular risks. There must be easier ways of earning a living. Did they discipline so much courage and talent towards feats of daring in a compulsive urge to receive acclaim at whatever cost? Was it enough knowing that the eyes of hundreds were riveted upon them for those few perilous moments? Or was it a sort of death wish, which in a way I shared a little, when driving the Porsche at 120 miles an hour?

'Well,' Jack said, 'I guess that's over. Those sure are brave men.'

'I'm just mad about them,' Babe said. 'I'm sorry it's over so soon. I wish they would do it again.' Her eyes were shining. Perhaps that was my answer: vicarious thrills were needed. In the end, it was a question of supply and demand.

'What are we going to see tomorrow night?' asked Babe, avid for kicks.

'It says here: "A human sacrifice before one of the great Aztec gods, which will conjure up memories of strange and ancient rituals".' Jack read out of a brochure.

'The Aztecs thought themselves to be the People of the Sun,' I informed them, 'and considered it their duty to offer the blood and heart of human sacrifices to the sun god. As many as twenty thousand people were slaughtered at a time, I believe, on a sacred feast day, the

50

hearts of the victims being carved out with a stone knife.'

'Wow! Nice people,' murmured the sister-in-law.

'I wonder how they'll do the heart cutting out bit,' mused Babe.

'Babe, honey, you are a ghoul.'

'Oh, I don't know, we all must have the killer instinct,' she answered coolly. 'Look how we swat flies. Cruelty is in all of us. Don't you agree, John?'

'Maybe,' I said lightly. The conversation made me uneasy.

Jack put an end to it. 'What's going to kill me is all these late nights. Let's go get some sleep.'

Jack was a good sort and I had become attached to him. He was considerate and patient and had the excellent manners of so many Americans. I bore with Babe's non-sense rather for his sake than for hers. I knew that he wanted me to be kind to her.

We were sitting in the shade of the open air bar with a drink the next day while the women were out shopping. Gazing over the sapphire bay, he was saying, 'Women are foolish creatures sometimes, so we have to look after them. But, boy, it's good to get away and do a bit of fishing. I have this log cabin in the mountains and the lake is full of fish. Wish it was nearer. We would leave the women to their shopping and you and me, we could just take off and go there. No talking, no shopping, no people – just fish. I go there whenever I can get away. Peaceful. Not for too long, mind. I like to get back to my wife and home; but it eases the strain. I guess we all need that. Why not come and stay sometime? You'd be very welcome.'

There was a part of me which would have liked to do just that; go to the log cabin with Jack and see if I could come to terms with myself. 'Peaceful,' he said. Oh, God, could I find peace that way?

'May I take a rain check?' I replied, American fashion. 'Nothing I would like better one day. If you visit England meanwhile, I hope you will come and meet my mother and see her English garden. I believe you would find a great deal to interest you in our way of life. I, too, fish in Devon sometimes.'

As I said it, I had a vivid picture of Maria on the cliffs, the wind blowing through her hair. Gulls were wheeling and crying their plaintive cries, and the sea was far below, green, with a sleepy swell on it. No, I would stop thinking of that now.

Restlessly, I felt I was wasting time in Acapulco; I resolved to return immediately to Mexico City and try to get to grips with the Plummers.

That evening, again sitting in an overcrowded restaurant, I broke the news of my imminent departure to my friends. Babe had come to the conclusion, she said, that I was in love, or maybe suffering from a broken heart. I smiled and shook my head silently, not wishing her to realize how near the truth she had got and yet how far from the real cause of my melancholy. She had now taken to holding my hand and looking at me sorrowfully. After all, she was not a bad sort either, and her absurd chatter had helped to distract me a little from my black brooding.

We bade each other affectionate good-byes in the morning. Babe and her sister-in-law kissed me. Jack and I, having exchanged addresses, vowed to meet again. We might. But in my experience holiday friendships sadly fade with the holiday.

There was a two-hour delay at the airport, which made me fidgety again, looking round to see if I was being followed. Though haunted in my thoughts by him, I had not, after all, met the grey man in Acapulco. Perhaps

52

Taxco had been a coincidence. Why then this persistent foreboding that I had not seen the last of him?

Anyway, after Mexico City, I was off to remote Cuzco, in Peru, and then to Machu Picchu. "The Lost City of the Incas". I looked forward to this splendid isolation, hoping it might help me to get things into a better perspective. Also, it would be a breather before the tumult of Rio in carnival, the final fling in my planned holiday.

The plane was announced and I was soon thankfully aboard.

Air travel bores me. It is not that I am scared; it just makes me uneasy to be completely in the power of others. I prefer to feel a steering wheel under my hand, make my own speed, see something of the land I am travelling through. Still, if flying is inevitable, I sighed, relax and enjoy it.

I ordered a drink, then settled in my seat with my yet unread thriller. Before long, my eyes glazed over the print and I was in that trancelike state, half dream, half reality, remembering . . .

She was blue, long and beautiful. I patted her affectionately: my Porsche.

'Come along, Maria,' I called impatiently, as she appeared through the front door, slung about with her last-minute packings. 'I want to get on the road before the traffic catches up with us.'

My mother had said on the Friday, when I drove her over to Lady Hetherington, together with all her gypsy props, 'I've brushed up my palmistry and have worked out a number of different fortunes to try out on my customers. I'm quite looking forward to it, you know.

Now take care, John darling. Don't go too fast in all that traffic, and leave some fish in the sea for the others.'

Mother was right. The roads to the West were full of traffic, but when we came to a motor-way, I would let the Porsche have her head and we flashed past everything in sight. Maria clutched her seat tight when we went over a hundred. She never cried, 'Be careful,' but once when I had gone on too long, she put her hand quietly on my thigh and said, 'I want you alive, John.'

So I was careful not to do it too often. My mother, too, disliked fast driving and I was used to considering my passengers. When alone, I could not go fast enough.

It was a good day for travelling, not too bright a sun, white clouds in the windswept sky, but no rain. Driving through Somerset, Maria would call out at times, 'Go slow, please, John. The countryside is so lovely.'

The rich red earth, green fields dotted with tranquil cattle, and Maria sitting beside me, filled me too with a deep contentment. Every now and again I would burst into song through sheer joy and Maria sometimes joined in. Our high spirits, our happiness at being together, touched everything we saw with beauty and excitement. We talked nonsense and laughed incessantly and the miles and hours melted away. At one point, I said to her, 'How come that your English is so perfect, darling? I know your ma is English, but tell me the rest.'

'Strange that I haven't told you before. Simply, father was in England working at the BBC during the war. He was broadcasting propaganda programmes to Greece, pumping them full of news and courage while they were occupied by the Nazis and dying of starvation by the thousand. They would all listen in, risking death to hear the news from their allies. Many were caught and tortured. Whole villages were burnt and people brutally put

54

to death, because of their stubborn resistance, and the help they gave to hidden English soldiers stranded in Greece. But that's all past history. He met my mother at the BBC. She was a secretary working in the translations section, and they married. I was born in England, you see, so have dual nationality. I was seven years old when my grandpa died some while after the war, and Father and Mother decided to go to Crete and take over the running of his hotel. It seems my grandma died of a broken heart, after seeing her younger son put to death in one of the round-ups. I never knew either of my Greek grandparents. Pity.'

We both fell silent while I digested the dramatic background of Maria's family. Maria was twenty-four now, so this was hearsay to her. Thus she was able to talk about it objectively.

Presently she went on, 'Anyway, we all speak English at home, even in Greece. My mother spoke no Greek and my Pa's English is excellent. Later, of course, Mother picked up some Greek and I went to school there and soon spoke it fluently. But we often came to England in the holidays, myself and my baby sister, to see my mother's mother and I would sometimes stay with Granny for the entire summer.'

'So you have an English granny living here?' I asked her, surprised.

'No, she died five years ago,' Maria said sadly.

By now we were speeding, but with caution, through the twisting country lanes of Devon, Maria exclaiming in amazement at the tall hedges hemming us in, the wild flowers and blackberries, the many birds and small animals that crossed our path.

'It's like another world,' she sighed. 'I wish we could go plopping down here in a pony and trap.'

'You mean: "A Surrey with a fringe on top" – I doubt that we would have made it from London.' I stopped and peered at a signpost, 'And in time for lunch, too,' I added triumphantly, pulling up at the end of the lane before the small country inn where I had booked. It was thatched, white-washed, the clematis blue on its brown oak beams; pink roses clutched at its walls.

Maria scrambled out and stretched contentedly, 'Clever John,' she said. 'I couldn't have done better myself.'

The air hostess arrived with some sort of luncheon. I managed to struggle through the best of it, and soon after we touched down. By the time I had reached my hotel back in Mexico City, reclaimed my luggage, unpacked and sorted out my cleaning chores, it had become too late to contact the Embassy that day.

I took the silver mask out and hung it on my wall. It would sustain me in my resolution to go and tackle the Plummers.

The next morning I was round at the Embassy offices bright and early. The secretary was busy – would I mind waiting? I waited, in a daze of anxiety. I still did not know what I would say to the Plummers. No doubt the words would come when I met them, or rather Mrs Plummer, if possible. Women were always more understanding in such matters.

Finally I was ushered into the secretary's office. She was a middle-aged woman, not unpleasant, but her manner, businesslike and brisk, was off-putting.

She said, 'I'm so sorry I've kept you waiting, Mr Devigne. I was on a long-distance call. I'm afraid I have disappointing news for you. Mr and Mrs Plummer came back two days ago and had to leave immediately for an urgent meeting in Washington. It was unexpected and sudden.'

I looked at her blankly, a deep sense of anti–climax slowly churning over inside me. I had keyed myself up to such a pitch for this meeting, and now it was not to be. I was speechless.

The secretary registered my consternation. She rustled her papers in embarrassment and said, 'I did mention to Mrs Plummer that you had called and she said she was sorry to have missed meeting you. Of course, if you left a message with me, I would make sure she received it. Or if there is anything I can do to help?'

Her question hung in the air, but I was still silent. I shrank from telling this woman what I wanted. Her detached manner was not intended to be unfriendly. It was merely the impersonal front of her business personality, but it did not invite confidences.

'Never mind. I'll write to Mrs Plummer,' I said at last. 'Thank you.' I rose and left her abruptly. Here I was, out on a limb again.

I wandered round the busy streets, taking nothing in, my mind seething, wondering what to do next.

I had come to Mexico City specifically to sound out Maria's previous employers, the Plummers: to see if they had heard anything from Maria's parents; to find out what repercussions there may have been to my actions; or just to break the terrible silence on Maria that I had lived in these past months.

When my gloom had deepened and my despair taken on the shape of illness, everyone had become worried over me back home, especially Edward, my partner, who realized that our practice was beginning to suffer under the strain.

Normally I was good at my work. I took a sympathetic interest in the troubles of my clients – and most clients came to me because of their troubles. It was not unlike being a psychiatrist; women sometimes wept before me while I offered hot coffee and comfort, and men, too, treated me as a sort of father figure, though I was usually younger than they. Their gratitude made me feel I was doing something worth while. I genuinely enjoyed helping my clients out of their tangles; pity I could do nothing about my own.

But the two months before my trip I had become almost unable to concentrate on the problems of others; the image of Maria constantly floated between me and those who sat facing me across my desk. Often I had not taken in a word they had said, and was obliged to ask them to write, putting it all down. Not unnaturally, they became increasingly bewildered and dissatisfied and went to Edward with their complaints. Finally, he tackled me over brandy after a dinner at his home.

'I've no intention of interfering in your affairs, John,' he had started tentatively, 'but I don't think it would be going too far to say you do not seem at all well. Clients have been remarking on it and Rosemary is quite worried. We both are. Maybe you are just tired and strained. You've not taken a proper holiday this summer. Why not have a few weeks off over Christmas and go to a hot clime? We are not so busy at the moment. I can easily manage your clients and Triksy can handle the conveyancing.' 'Triksy' was Trikering, our chief clerk, older than either of us, older than the hills, and invaluable on conveyancing.

True that I had not taken a long holiday that summer. Maria and I could not both leave Mother at the same time and I did not want a holiday without her.

Rosemary, who had removed herself tactfully, then came in with the coffee.

'I've been suggesting to John that he goes off to some exotic hot place for a rest,' Edward said to her – as though she did not know!

'Where would you choose, John? If you went?'

'Mexico City,' I answered promptly. Because I had been turning over in my mind for some time the best way to approach the Plummers.

'*That* is some choice,' said Rosemary. 'I've always had a hankering to go to Peru,' she added wistfully.

'Peru, too, then,' I humoured her.

'And while you're about it,' Rosemary was getting excited, 'you must go to Rio. The carnival is on soon and ever since seeing that marvellous film "Black Orpheus", I've thought how terrific it would be to participate in it. Why not go if you are practically on the spot?'

'Why not, indeed?' I had entered into the spirit of the thing. The brandy must have been a strong one.

After that, we all sat down with maps and started to work out a rough itinerary, backwards from the carnival. I wanted to spend Christmas at home with Mother, anyway. Rosemary promised to visit her every week while I was away. A solid middle-aged woman was looking after her at the time, dull but reliable. Once the decision was taken, I felt almost light-hearted.

The next day I went to a travel agent and booked it all. I knew Mother would be pleased. She had been urging me to take a rest for some time.

In fact, when I told her the following week-end that I would be going to the South Americas for a three weeks' holiday around the middle of January, she had said, 'About time, too. Wish I was coming with you. South America is a continent that has always intrigued me. The only thing that would put me off would be the thought of the tarantulas.'

'Darling mother, I shan't be cleaving my way through a jungle. I expect modern hotels have dispersed their tarantulas long ago.'

'I do hope so,' mused my mother, 'even if it has disturbed the balance of nature.' We had touched on one of her favourite topics.

By now back in my hotel room, I felt lost. Having failed to contact the Plummers, it seemed pointless to have come to Mexico in the first place. However, my so-called holiday had been pre-booked and pre-paid. What reason could I give for returning home at this point?

In a kind of weary daze, I picked up the phone to the hotel desk and asked them to confirm my flight to Lima. It would be leaving at six o'clock next morning, they informed me.

I took down the mask and packed it away. From now on I would keep it in my suitcase; it stirred up in me too much guilt and sorrow.

CHAPTER EIGHT

Miraculously, my preoccupation with Maria left during the next few days.

Waking at four in the morning to make the airport in time for my six o'clock plane, I arrived to find that the aircraft to Lima was not just delayed – but lost! I wondered, vaguely, whether it had been hi-jacked. None of the officials appeared to know, or even care. A great many agitated passengers with appointments were milling about in angry frustration. Some were creating a furious fuss. I tagged on to see what would happen. Nothing happened. Except that we were reluctantly given vouchers for breakfast in the restaurant; just a ruse to get rid of us, because when we came back to the airline desk it was closed and the official birds had flown!

By now I had become attached to a young Canadian, who seemed to know the ropes. He said, 'You must switch to a more reliable air-line.' Alas, it being still only seven o'clock, there was a long wait for their offices to open, and the airport, bitterly cold in the early morning, offered no comfort. By nine o'clock I had begun to feel the combined strain of angry argument, uncertainty, and lack of sleep.

Fortunately, one of the other lines, in fact, did find me a place. But *their* plane would not be leaving for Lima until six p.m., arriving around midnight. What to do till then? I decided to take a room at a nearby hotel and slipped gladly between the sheets for a couple of hours sleep. The rest of the day I spent glued to my still unread thriller – at last. The tangible frustration of the delayed flight had cleared my mind of its greater preoccupations, and I found it possible to relax and concentrate on my book. In it the murderer, who killed his victim by accident, remained undetected, and the final chapter finished with his seeking another victim. Can murder truly become an acquired taste, I mused?

I had cabled the travel agents in Lima and was met by a courier on my arrival, just after midnight. On the way to my hotel, he informed me that my flight to Cuzco was booked for seven o'clock that same morning – so that only a few hours later found me again at an airport awaiting a plane!

This time the delay was a short one, since the plane had to be flown through a narrow pass between high mountains while conditions were favourable. Cuzco is eleven thousand feet high in the Andes, and the weather there swiftly changeable. As we came safely through the pass, I had an impression of a brooding mountain range with rounded sugar loaf tops; there were deep, shadowed canyons in between.

My hotel, an unpretentious inn, had a notice on its stripped-pine walls, warning the newly-arrived to take a rest until they had become accustomed to the altitude. Weary with constant travel, I thought this advice excellent.

I took to my new surroundings and spent the next three days happily roaming the mountains. Clouds drifted constantly around them; there were showers, but it was not very cold. Snow gleamed only on those at 15,000 feet; the rest were green. I gazed around me:

green, green, disappearing into the distance much further than the eye could see. Mountains on mountains on mountains. They had, as I had anticipated, a calming effect on me. Their vastness put one's own puny self and actions into a diminished perspective.

Indians with light coppery skins farmed the fertile valleys. I met them often on the slopes, guarding their herds of llama and alpaca. For the first time on this trip I used my camera. The women in vivid multiple skirts, a kind of trilby hat on their heads, would shyly cover their faces in superstitious fear. They carried a small wooden spindle on which they constantly spun llama wool. Their children, fat and sweet, with glowing cheeks and big brown eyes, ran in and out amongst the long-necked animals. No doubt they were poor and exploited, but their gentle dignity gave them an almost noble look in this magnificient environment.

At nights, tired out by my explorations and the high altitude, I slept like a log. Not even once did I get the recurring nightmare about Maria. It was as if some kind fate had decided I had had enough agony of mind for the time being, and that these three days were to be a soothing interval, building up strength for what was to come.

The excursion to Machu Picchu was planned for the next day. Several groups of tourists had been flown in and we were all going on the single track railway in one big crowd tomorrow.

It was drizzling in the morning but the light was still bright. There was a tremendous bustle getting us all away early to the train, and then started the ride to what my guide book proudly described as: 'Possibly the most beautiful spot in the world'. I have travelled enough to be very wary of guide-book splurge. Not only is beauty very much in the eye of the beholder, but this same beholder (certainly in my case), is at the mercy of his moods and, of course, the weather.

There were four carriages to the rail-car, all filled with tourists. The seats were comfortable, fortunately, as it was to be a three-hour journey. We first climbed the mountains by a series of switchbacks, then made a spectacular plunge down, down into a wide valley; the gleaming glaciers were above us, the Urubamba River below, a fierce, tumbling torrent, filled with rapids. The scenery became increasingly wild, tropical and jungly. The rail-track ran by the river, between high canyons. There was no road, no other approach to this remote place.

I was gazing mesmerized out of the window at the gaunt mountains, the exotic vegetation, the swirling, angry torrent, and by some trick of imagination, the scene dissolved into the smooth green lawns of a calm English garden: there was a duck pond, with two ducks . . .

It was the view from the window of our Devon inn. Maria and I were in the dining-room. We were having a glutonous lunch; generous helpings, dollops of cream. We ate ravenously. We had left early that morning, and it had been a long drive. Maria made a puffed-out face. 'I've eaten enough for a week.'

'Don't you believe it,' I said. 'There are the delights of a Devonshire tea to follow later this afternoon. You can't escape that.'

'Well, I must have some exercise in between. Let's go for a walk – or a swim. You have remembered your swim things?'

'I have.'

Maria burst out laughing. 'What's so funny?' I asked.

'As I said that, a crazy situation I was once in flashed through my mind.'

'Well? Tell me.'

'You won't like it. Nikos comes into it.'

She spoke of him quite casually now and, though I was secretly jealous, I thought it best for neither of us to be inhibited about her past. 'Come on. Let's hear it,' I said.

'Well, one very hot day, Nikos and I decided to play truant in the afternoon and took off to this seaside place, some miles outside Athens. It is a fabulous spot: the pines grow round a sandy beach, quite deserted, and it's possible to bathe in the nude. We did not even bother to go and fetch our swim things. We drove the car down a sort of dirt track off the road, as far as we could, then walked through the trees to the sea. We threw our clothes on the sand and plunged in. The sea was wonderful I remember, clear, like silk on the skin. We swam over to some rocks and lay on them, diving in and out. We must have been away an hour before we swam back. When we walked on to our beach, our clothes were gone. We couldn't believe it at first and searched around for ages – but they had gone. Some peeping Tom had pinched them. We walked back to the car – Nikos never locked the door in such a place – but there was nothing in it, nothing – not even a towel. I got out again to see if I could make some sort of cover with pine branches and was delighted to find my bra and pants, thrown on to the ground, not far from the car. The thief must have had second thoughts on those!'

'Such delicacy!' I murmured.

Maria laughed. 'It showed *some* consideration. He can't have been *all* bad.'

'Perhaps they didn't fit,' I suggested.

'Anyway,' Maria continued, 'here we were: me in my

bra and pants – Nikos stark naked. No money, because Nikos's wallet and my bag had been stolen too, and the last straw was, when Nikos tried to start the car, we found the wheels spinning in the sandy track and it wouldn't move!'

'Curiouser and curiouser. What did you do?'

'You may well ask. One of us had to go for help. We knew there was an army camp about a mile away and lorries with soldiers often went by on the road. But I didn't relish the thought of trying to stop a lorryload of soldiers in a bra and pants, and Nikos, too, was fearful of appearing stark naked on a main road.'

'Well, I expect the Greeks have a word for that, too,' I quipped.

'As a matter of fact, it is forbidden to bathe in the nude – though many break this silly law when in a discreet place. We beat our brains out for a solution. Nikos even tried to get my stretch pants on – we were in stitches by then – so were the pants, nearly. He soon gave that up. So I decided I would have to go. Nikos tore a pine branch down and I held it in front of me like a shield and stood in the main road, feeling a cross between Lady Godiva and an early Christian martyr. It wasn't long before two lorries, full of soldiers, came into view. You can imagine the cat-calls and whistles, but they stopped at my signal and one of the officers jumped down; when I told him my story briefly, he stripped off his shirt and put it, hot and sweaty, round my shoulders. It was a gallant act. I wish I could have knighted him on the spot, like a queen.' Maria stopped, her eyes bright with laughter, looking into the past.

'So, did this have a happy ending?'

'Oh yes, of course, the soldiers came to our rescue then. Half a dozen of them almost lifted the car bodily out

66

of the sand on to the road. One of them gave Nikos his underpants and the officer said I could send his shirt back later. And that's how we returned to Athens. Nikos in the borrowed underpants – me in a sweaty shirt.' She chuckled. 'I sent it back washed and ironed and with a tinsel star pinned to it. I hope he got the message.'

I laughed with her and it *was* funny. It was also disburbing – the picture of Maria naked, with her previous lover. I was consumed with jealousy and wanted to possess her at once.

'Maria, let's have a snooze first, then go for a walk.' I reached for her hand.

She pulled it out of reach. 'No. Walk first, snooze after – or we'll never go,' she said firmly.

So we went. Towards the sea. It was about a mile down a lane, splattered with cow dung. We met a herd of black and white cows; Maria touched their steamy flanks as we wove our way through them. Everything delighted her, especially the abundance of wild flowers and the views over the curving downs to the distant moors.

We broke through a hedge and there was the cliff path, the sea still a long way below. Cornfields were all around us. It had become hot and we sat down to cool off. I put my arm around Maria and kissed her. She trembled in that delicious way and I undid her blouse and kissed her again. Her heart was beating fast under my hand and I was mad to have her. I dragged her down. The high hedge was behind us and tall grasses hid us from view.

'No, John,' she protested. 'Let's wait till we get back to the hotel.'

'Damn the hotel!'

'Someone might see us.'

'Only the odd seagull. Come on, darling. Now.' I

jammed my coat under her head and fell on top of her. Gradually her protests got weaker. Her lips were soft and hot and she was breathing rapidly. I looked at her a moment, lying there, disarrayed, flushed, eyes clouded with desire. I needed desperately to oust the lingering unpleasantness of her story: she and her student naked; worse, in the intimacy of laughter over a shared experience. It was poison; I *had* to rid her body and mind of its previous intruder.

'You are mine, mine, mine,' I ground out between clenched teeth, as I went deep into her beautiful body. The earth and sky seemed to move in with me; we were bound together in one elemental, life-giving force.

'John, my darling, yes.' Her voice was hoarse, pleading. A great strength surged through me and again and again I possessed her fiercely. There was a tumult in my head, of rushing winds, seas breaking on rocks, gulls screaming and Maria's moans, as she clutched me, struggling, crying out, lost.

Only when it was over did the sounds die away to their normal levels: the sea a distant soughing, the gulls' cries faint, the wind a gentle breeze just moving the tall grasses.

Maria lay still, her arms flung wide; her hair a black tangle on the dry grass – her eyes closed . . .

It hurt too much to think; I shook my head to free myself from the memory of that fatal afternoon.

Focusing back on to the life bustling around me, I noticed, on the seats parallel with mine on the other side of the compartment, a slim, black-haired girl with her two children – little boys around five and seven. Their father was explaining about Machu Picchu to them out of an illustrated guide book. He was dark and lean and about my age. Like a bright burst of sunshine in the greyness of my misery, I saw a sudden picture of myself with Maria as my wife and our children sitting beside us. But the image quickly faded, and I shivered. How could such happiness ever be mine?

When the train stopped, the drive from the bottom of the valley was along a road so steep, I counted thirteen hairpin bends. At last we reached Machu Picchu, the fantastic hide-away, last refuge of the Incas. The Spaniards had not found it, nor indeed anyone since, until some sixty years ago when it was discovered by an American explorer.

At first sight, the drama of this place stunned me. The peak of the mountain towered darkly over the saddle on which the Incas had built their houses and temples, and hundreds of terraces fell away steeply down towards the raging river below. The remains of the City, built of huge blocks of white granite, were in various stages of reconstruction, but much had survived as first built, gaunt and forbidding.

A fine rain was falling and black clouds hung over the vast range of mountains. Perhaps it was this, or my own dark thoughts, that filled me with unease. I could not help wondering about the slave labour that must have toiled up these almost vertical slopes with the huge blocks of stone necessary to build the homes of the more privileged Incas. I saw the altar on which sacrifices were made to the Sun God, and wondered again how many young men and women had been cruelly slaughtered upon it. I am sensitive to atmosphere, I know, and looking around at the brooding immensity of the surroundings, the deep ravines, the raging river, I felt shut in and unhappy, as those Incas must have felt – trapped, hidden, fearing discovery by their Spanish conquerors, living here by necessity rather than choice, forcing food out of the harsh mountain with constant terracing and endless labour. It was not a happy ambience – to me, anyway. However, I took out my camera to get a few slides of the awesome scene.

Taking photographs is not one of my hobbies. I point the camera and hope for the best. All the same, I'm fussy about composition. I'd had the thing glued to my eye for some time, turning this way and that, when into the shot walked the grey man.

It was barely a week since I had seen him in Taxco, but it seemed much longer and I had almost convinced myself that I had imagined him, or at worst, thrown him off my trail. He must have picked it up again, else what could he possibly be doing in this remote place on exactly the same day as I?

The shock had made my hands shake, I noticed with surprise, keeping the camera to my eye while I took a better look at him. His lean face had two deep lines etched down each cheek and there was a small moustache. His pale eyes glittered a little as he stared back at me, unsmiling, grim.

I could not bare the stare, so I clicked the camera and turned away, quickly rejoining my group like a sheep returning to the protection of the fold, or rather, up here, like a llama. The sturdy Peruvian guide who spoke such good English was talking about the wonders of the Inca buildings, showing the remains of some perfectly jointed wall. I was not listening and waited impatiently to break in with my question.

'Who is that man?' at last I asked.

'What man?' He turned to follow my outstretched arm.

The grey man had by now faded into his own group. He had the quality of a shadow. One moment strong, menacing; the next, completely invisible.

'He's tall, thin, grey and has a moustache,' I said rather wildly.

The guide looked at me, puzzled at my anxiety. 'I'm afraid I wouldn't know if he's not in my group.'

'It doesn't matter. I thought it was someone I had met before.'

'Why don't you ask him yourself, then?'

'Of course I will. When next I see him.' And I told myself I would do just that. Go up and tackle him. But what would I say? Who are you? Are you following me? If so, why?

Better to ignore him. If I played it cool, haunting me would get him nowhere.

I slipped away to the coach which had brought me and, losing myself behind a paper, waited for the return of the rest of my group. On the train journey back I sat tensely in a corner. The remote mountains no longer offered sanctuary; I was now anxious to get back to the protective anonymity of a crowded city.

My guide arranged for me to be on the early morning plane to Lima.

Once arrived there, I went at once to reclaim my luggage left in a Lima hotel, and fished out my itinerary to remind myself of dates. I was surprised to find that the carnival in Rio was starting today. It had caught up with me. Waiting around for the Plummers' return, plus the delayed flights, had eaten into my time.

By a stroke of luck, I managed to find a seat on an afternoon plane. My hotel in Rio had, of course, been booked well in advance.

I got to the airport early. No one appeared to be

following me and I felt confident that my next move would shake the grey man off for good. For by now I was quite convinced that he *was* following me; surely the long arm of coincidence could not have stretched as far as Machu Picchu?

Even assuming that he succeeded in tracing my flight to Rio, it seemed now to me that I would be lost there, merging into the riotous crowds of the carnival, and he would find it well nigh impossible to pick up my scent.

At least, that was my optimistic hope as I waited impatiently for my plane: late, I was told unconcernedly – yes, it was late!

I arrived in Rio at about eleven o'clock that night, after a seven-hour journey.

CHAPTER NINE

The City was already in fiesta, judging by the illuminations and deviations. The taxi driver cursed in Portuguese and drove with the sort of dedicated determination to outdo all others on the road, usually associated with bandits in a film chase. When I protested once at a near crash, he silenced me with such an imperious gesture, I subsided, crushed. I was to find this crazy driving normal practice amongst the taxis here.

My hotel was well placed; right on the road by Copacabana beach, about a hundred yards from the sea. They gave me a pleasant room on the second floor. I turned up the air conditioning and threw off my sticky clothes. The temperature, even so late at night, must have been in the 80s. There was a large bottle of iced mineral water in my room. I drank the lot. Then, having dutifully unpacked my suits, I fell on to the bed and into a deep sleep.

I suppose I must have outslept my exhaustion, when the cacophonous noises, which had no doubt been going on for some time, finally penetrated my dreams. Where was I? I stumbled to the window and below me saw a long procession winding in and out of the busy road. An improvised Samba band: some were banging drums, some shaking caracas, others were clashing together frying pans, saucepan lids, any old kitchen utensil. It was a

73

raggle taggle mob; dancing, singing, whistling. A few fireworks banged and sizzled. I looked at my watch and was astonished to see it was 3 a.m. For a moment, I considered slipping on a shirt and trousers and joining the riot, but the heat and the whisky I had drunk on the plane had drained my energy, and I fell back on to the bed. Time enough. This was only the first night, a warming up for the big nights to follow: tomorrow and the next day.

The noise was appalling. When the procession went by, following cars hooted – and more processions followed the cars. About five o'clock it became quieter and sleep blissfully overcame me. The sun, streaming hotly through the blinds, finally woke me. It was ten o'clock.

My first thought, after orange juice and coffee, was for a swim. The temperature must have been in the 90s and still going up. I scorned the hotel pool and made across the burning sands to the sea.

On Bank holidays anywhere in the world, especially by the sea, is crowded. On Copacabana, had I had the proverbial pin, it would have been a problem to put it between the people. I stumbled my way through to the water's edge and there further disillusion awaited me. Huge curling breakers were crashing on the shore. I noticed the crowds were just standing on the fringe of the surf, splashing themselves with water. This was not for me. Nor would I be so foolish as to tackle such savage seas, strong swimmer though I am. Defeated, I picked my way back again over the bodies on the sand to the hotel swimming pool.

The heat was too great for sight-seeing, but I bought tickets from the hotel desk for the procession of the Samba schools that night. I was looking forward with some excitement to participating in the carnival.

There was a gradual crescendo of noise around our hotel as darkness fell. I finished my dinner and another lunatic taxi driver hurtled me towards the centre of town, escaping death by a whisker, over and over. I was thankful when he said he could go no further because traffic was barred and I must find my own way to the stands.

It was no easy task. Vast crowds were concentrated in this area of town reserved for the principal carnival festivities. I could not so much walk through them, as drift along with them. There was no great hurry, however. The Samba processions went on for several hours. The stands were somewhere – many of these people were making their way towards them. Others had formed processions of their own. Some were in fancy dress, some in light summer clothes, but all wore as little as possible in view of the heat. Their bodies gleamed as they rattled and banged their instruments; dancing and singing and waving their arms about. It was infectious, and I found myself joining in a procession Sambaing to a catchy tune which was the present rave. There were cries of 'Ooh, la, la' every so often, and I joined in, surprised at the sound of my voice. A paper whistle was blown in my face and turning, I saw a pretty dark girl laughing at me. My first impression was that she looked like Maria. She blew the whistle at me again. Absolutely spontaneously, I put my arm round her waist and kissed her, full on the mouth. She was delighted, caught my hand, and in a flash I was Sambaing with her and crying 'Ooh, la, la' like a mad thing. It was a release. Since Babe and her crowd, I had kept to myself. The time had come for some fun.

The stands came into view. I showed the girl my tickets. 'You come with me?' I asked, miming my words. She answered in English, 'I come, Americano.'

'No, not American – English,' I protested, firmly.

'American, English?' She shrugged as though imply-
ing: what's the difference? 'Come, I take you,' and still
holding hands, we broke from the procession and made
our way through the excited crowds to the stands.

Once we had found our seats, I had a good look at my
girl. She had none of Maria's class; the intelligence and
poise were lacking, but she was small-boned, with dark
hair to her shoulders, and pretty enough. Her brown
eyes, almost black, laughed up at me as she put her arm
through mine and snuggled close. It was very comforting.

The noise and general tumult all around was now
drowned by the more specific rhythm of the Sambas,
played by the various 'schools', as the mile-long procession came into view. The crowds in the stands roared
their approbation as each of the schools approached.

The schools varied from groups of one hundred to one
thousand men and women mixed. Some wore elaborate
clothes: beaded crinolines, wigs and Monsieur Beaucaire
outfits, contrasting with near-nude girls in spangles and
feathers, and men in tinsel slips. They exuded an astound-
ing vitality, whirling and twirling to their loud bands. In
their exuberance, men turned cartwheels as though on a
spindle and girls shook all over in a kind of belly dance
frenzy. Samba, Samba, Samba: the exhilarating mixture
of African and Portuguese, both in the music and the
people, was tremendously exciting, and I felt caught up
in the general fever.

There came the point where the procession was about
centre of our stand, stretching for a dazzling half mile
each way. The noise had reached a frenetic pitch. My girl
knew the people in the Samba school abreast of us. She
called out excitedly to them by name. They were on the

'ooh, la, la,' bit and we both stood up clapping and shouting. They waved and shouted back, but went on Sambaing proudly, without altering their tempo. They knew they were the star turn. When they had passed, the rest seemed an anti-climax and we both wanted to leave the stand. It was now nearly 3 a.m.

The streets were still thronged with amateur groups and their improvised Samba bands, and we joined in a procession, dancing along, I holding my girl's hand. 'What's your name?' I shouted, hugging her in a quick embrace.

'Anita,' she shouted back. 'Yours?'

'Simon,' I said. Some cautious instinct prompted this. It was my second name.

'I'm thirsty.' I made a drinking motion. 'Let's go somewhere to drink.'

'I take you.' She led me down a side street to an all-night café. It was packed with people, but at least the noisy bands were now in the distance. I managed to find a table inside where it was quieter. I wanted a chance to get to know my girl.

'Anita,' I said. 'A pretty name – pretty like you.' Most women like this kind of corny compliment and Anita was no exception. She dimpled and said, 'I like your name, too, Simon. You are tourist?'

I nodded. 'And you? You work here?'

'Yes. I am assistant in photographs. Is big journal.' She mentioned the name of an illustrated Brazilian paper. 'We are holiday now, but will be *mucho, mucho* work when go back.' She made a vigorous shaking gesture with her hand, emphasizing her words.

'Anita, while you are on holiday, will you show me round? Will you spend tomorrow with me?'

She countered this with another question. 'Do you go

to the big Opera Ball tomorrow?'

'I don't know. Would you like to go?'

Her face lit up and she flashed her charming smile at me. 'Yes. Yes, please. I like.'

'Well, then, I'll take you. What is this ball?'

'Is big, big ball of carnival. All peoples, rich, important, go. They were beautiful clotheses.'

'But I have no beautiful clotheses. I have no fancy dress.' I was wearing a short-sleeved silk shirt and a pair of light cotton trousers and they were sticking to me with the heat.

'I fix it. You put same on tomorrow, because is too hot. Is easy fix it for you. OK?' She was so eager to go, she was determined to make it all right. I thought the hotel would give me some advice on what to wear.

'OK. I'll ask the hotel to get me tickets. I expect they can.'

'What is your hotel?' she asked a little anxiously.

Again I was cautious and only gave a half truth. 'I am on the Copacabana,' and I named a hotel a few hundred yards from mine.

'Is big hotel,' she said, satisfied. 'You get tickets, but very, very expensive.' She made the shaking gesture with her hand again.

Though I am not extravagant by nature (except when it comes to acquiring beautiful things), I am given to certain reckless bursts if carried away by the occasion. This was such an occasion.

'Come on then, Anita. Drink up and I'll take you home. It's nearly four o'clock. Is your apartment near here?' I asked carefully.

'Is over there,' she said vaguely, waving in front of her. 'My cousin live too, there. But I not go still. I will meet my friends to another café.'

78

'Well, I'll put you on your way to this café.' She rose obediently and we went into the street, which was quieter now. Some of the revellers must have drifted away, although the carnival went on till dawn.

I pulled her into a dark doorway and kissed her good night. She submitted, giggling a little, but when I became more ardent, she pushed me away. 'No. No. Tomorrow – after we go dancing,' she said, smiling invitingly.

I was not sure if it was a promise or a carrot being dangled. I didn't want to frighten her away, however, so I said, 'That's a promise, Anita. I shall keep you to it.' Then I made a date to meet her the next afternoon, around 3 o'clock, on the terrace of the hotel I had named. She was obliged to lunch with her family, she said, but would take me sight-seeing and shopping in the afternoon.

'I will get tickets for the Opera Ball at the hotel in the morning,' I reassured her. I had forgotten it was morning already.

'You are nice Americano-English.' She smiled. 'I'm mad about you.' I heard in this the echo of some 'Americano' admirer, and wondered, a little cynically, how far she went with them all.

By the time I had found a taxi, I was so tired that I kept dropping off to sleep on the dare-devil drive back to my hotel. All the same, before going to bed, I made the night porter promise to find me tickets for tomorrow's ball. The price knocked me sideways, but I had made up my mind. I knew: no ball, no Anita, and I was sufficiently excited by her to make the gesture.

At three o'clock the next day, I was sitting on the terrace of the chosen hotel, anxiously waiting. I had the tickets to the Opera ball in my pocket; surely they were

79

burning a hole in it – they had cost so much! Had it not been for Anita, I would certainly not have gone, and now I was beginning to wonder if she would turn up.

At 3.30, I saw her walking calmly towards the terrace, looking cool and girlish in a sun dress. Her dark hair swung on her bare shoulders. Though it was neither as long nor as black as Maria's, it was that which reminded me of her.

I rose and waved and she came up to me and stood on tiptoe to kiss me lightly on both cheeks. 'You have the tickets?' she asked at once.

Smugly, I took them out of my pocket and slapped them on the table. She picked them up eagerly to make sure, and clasped them to her in an extravagant gesture. 'You are a wonderful boy. We have together a wonderful time. I take you later to a good jeweller. He is my friend. He make you special price.'

I'll bet, I thought. The price would more likely have a bit tagged on as a commission for Anita.

How could I ever have identified her with my gentle, undemanding Maria? This girl was a little gold-digger; that was becoming clear. But she had a pert nose and big mouth and her eyes, though at times calculating, could look merry enough. She had a lively personality and flirting with her cheered me up.

'Where are we going now? I'm in your hands,' I said.

'Going Corcovado,' she said firmly. 'You must see the Christos.' So we took the taxi I had hired in advance and went to the mountain overlooking Rio, its summit crowned by the huge stone figure of Christ. We passed coachloads of other tourists on the way. Such mass rubber-necking always depresses me; however, having come so far, we plodded up the steps to the gigantic Christ, arriving at the top breathless and dripping with

80

perspiration. It was worth it for the strange surrealist quality of the view spread out before us.

The coastline swept in and out with great curving beaches, and beyond were innumerable islands – islands of dark, conical-shaped mountains. The pointed peaks, stretching to infinity, looked like tall witch's hats, brooding together, sitting in conclave on the deep blue sea.

I said to Anita, 'Have you visited the islands? What are they like?'

She shrugged. 'Some good. But some not so good visit.'

'Why?' I asked.

'One has wood and many tarantulas grow – no, you say breed – there.'

'Tarantulas?' I remembered my mother's fears.

'Yes. Some peoples, they go for a picnic, leave boat and go into the woods for shade. The tarantulas come out and attack them. Some escape and get into boat – but, bad, bad.'

'What a horrible story! What happened?'

'I think soldiers go over and burn the woods and tarantulas too. Look,' she cried, bored with the subject, 'down there you can just see yacht of Texan millionaire. I know. I work on the photos for my paper.'

This was the first time I was to hear her pointing out the celebrities she knew, indirectly. She was very interested in the famous and rich.

Presently, becoming restless with my filming, she suggested again, 'You want we go shopping to my friend now? He make you special price.'

I allowed her to lead me to her jeweller. His special price had better be good.

The owner of the shop greeted Anita warmly, sizing me up and carefully for wealth. Bald, perspiring and anxious, he produced tray after tray of gems. The stones were beautiful. I knew a little about their value and picked out a chunky, carved aquamarine as a fob for my mother's chain. I mused over some citrine cuff links for Edward. A bit fancy perhaps, but I bought them. Anita kept trying on a white topaz ring.

It looks like diamond,' she said, rather wistfully, flashing her hand about to catch the light.

'How much is it?' I asked. The man named a ridiculously low price – only a few dollars. So I said. 'Anita, please accept it as a little present.'

She didn't waste time protesting. 'Thank you, Simon. So much generous you are,' she purred.

Realizing I had nothing for Edward's children, I got two silver charm bracelets for the girls. I must remember to get something, somewhere, for the three-year old, John.

I saw the shop owner look at Anita once or twice as though to say: Shall I bleed this sucker? But she put her arm through mine protectively, indicating, I suppose, that I was not a bad chap. So maybe I got a fair deal after all.

Once outside again, I stopped at a kiosk selling carnival fantasies and chose an amusing mask. It would help as a prop tonight and little Johnnie might enjoy it back home.

'That's it, then,' I said to Anita. 'Let's go for a drink. All that shopping's made me thirsty.'

We sat in a café and both had a beer. Anita, delighted with her ring, kept admiring it. I thought it the psychological moment to cash in some goodwill. 'Shall I come and collect you from your apartment on the way to the Ball?' I asked.

'No,' she said quickly. 'My cousin still there then. She does not know I go and she will be jealous. I meet you outside Opera. But,' she added, with a coy look, 'you can take me home after.'

'Will your cousin be gone?'

'Sure. She will be at carnival.'

Let's hope so, my impious thoughts were running. Well, we would find a way, provided she was willing. I was quite relaxed and for the first time in a long while, unworried.

Anita was anxious to go home and try on her fancy dress outfit for that night. We made a rendezvous for 11.30. The Ball did not get going until after midnight but Anita said it would take us half an hour to get in. We would be queuing up with thousands of celebrities, she reminded me, simmering with excitement in anticipation of mingling with the mighty!

I gave her a kiss as I put her in a taxi. She hugged me, thrilled. And I was happy, I told myself, living in the present, blotting out my dark thoughts that rose to the surface in spite of all my efforts to suppress them, like bubbles from a poisonous well – the well of my unhappiness.

CHAPTER TEN

Anita saw me first at the rendezvous. 'Hey, Simon,' she called. 'Is me. Look, you like my fancy dress?'

It was a non-dress almost. A wisp of a straw skirt and the briefest of bras in bright red. A garland of brilliant paper flowers went down to her waist, and behind her ear she had tucked a real hibiscus bloom. Her body was sun-tanned and she looked vivacious and most desirable – a bon-bon done up in bright ribbon.

'You are delicious,' I said. 'Why don't we just stay here and dance cheek-to-cheek all night?'

She laughed, delighted, knowing it was just a joke. Nothing short of murder would have stopped her now from attending the privileged Ball.

We queued up, as she had predicted, in a half-mile queue, while each ticket was examined minutely, to avoid fakes and gate-crashers. I had fixed the mask on the back of my head, so that I had a face both sides and it looked amusingly grotesque that way. That was my only concession to fancy dress. Otherwise, I was again in a short-sleeved silk shirt and cotton trousers. I noticed some elaborate outfits but mostly people were dressed with the heat in mind. The temperature was near to ninety, even now.

Great crowds had gathered behind the railings of the gardens to gawk at the 'quality' going to the Ball, or rather those who had enough money to squander this way. It was the playground of the rich. Anita preened herself at having at last successfully crashed this money barrier.

The Opera House was already packed when we were finally admitted. Normally seating two thousand people, with the seats removed, it was reckoned that five to seven thousand could be squeezed in. Tonight it seemed they would shortly have twice that number, judging by the continuous stream pouring through the doors.

The finals of the fancy dress parade were just over, and as we pushed our way into the main hall one of the bands burst into a Samba.

Anita and I went on to the big dance floor, soon crowded with jostling, Sambaing people. She knew many of the internationally wealthy and famous by sight and kept pointing them out: the British Ambassador, a Mexican film star, an oil king. She was a dancing 'Who's Who'.

As the tempo increased and more and more people forced themselves on to the floor, it became impossible to dance in couples and crocodiles were formed. I held Anita's waist, some bosomy blond held mine. We were all going round and round in great circles, weaving and Sambaing, singing and shouting, 'Oo-la-la!' You could feel the excitement spreading – it was palpable, hot, voluptuous in its abandon. Young men threw off their shirts, exposing brown chests gleaming with perspiration, and beautiful women, wearing extravagant head-dresses and very little else, stood on chairs, swinging their hips to the Samba, throwing their hands about. The two bands went on and on, each taking over from the other without a second's break.

I do not know how long it was before our crocodile

moved upstairs. By now the place was pulsing with a single heartbeat, pounding in a joyous freedom. I broke Anita away to view the spectacle from the balconies.

The spotlights shone on the glittering mass below: scarlet and gold, wild outfits, glistening bodies and waving hands, all moving exultantly to one compulsive rhythm.

I stood there spellbound.

Anita plucked my arm, bringing me out of my trance.

'Simon, I am thirsty. Shall we go to bar?'

'Of course, Anita. Me, too.' I realized for the first time that my shirt was soaked through.

The bars were hopelessly inadequate. Hundreds of thirsty people pushing and clamouring for attention. It was like several theatre first nights rolled into one. Driven to cheating and pushing myself, I eventually secured a large Scotch and soda and a bottle of champàgne, mainly for Anita. We sat on some stone steps leading to one of the Exit doors, now firmly barred against gate crashers. I wondered uneasily what would happen in a fire.

I drank my whisky thirstily, then said to Anita, 'Wait here a moment. I'm going to look around for some spot where we might sit in greater comfort to drink our champagne.'

I moved away into the main hall and saw yet another great crocodile of people coming down the wide staircase, singing and swaying. Fascinated, I stopped again to stare at their antics, when something caught my eye. I looked more carefully and I believe my mouth dropped open in astonishment. He was there, higher up on the staircase – the grey man, dressed in black. The severe black outfit had made me hesitate for a moment, but I knew his gaunt face well enough by now to have recognized him, even had he been disguised in scarlet like the devil. He looked straight back at me as was his habit, and then incredibly, it seemed that he waved – or was he pointing me out to someone?

I did not stop to see. My blood count must have risen alarmingly. I felt dizzy for a moment, then hot and cold. Beads of perspiration broke out all over me. Turning away blindly, I almost stumbled to the bar only a few yards away.

'Anita,' I said abruptly, 'it's too hot here. I'm going.'

'Going?' Her voice was shocked. 'But peoples are still arriving. Look.'

Sure enough, people were even now streaming in through the front door, facing us. The thousands in the Opera House would shortly be a million at this rate.

'All the more reason to go. It's too crowded.'

'But, Simon, I have not finished champagne.' Her voice was tearful. She had got through most of the bottle, in fact.

'Finish it quickly if you want to come with me. I'm going out to get some air.'

I thought for a moment she was going to throw it in my face. But she gulped it down and as I strode out of the door, I heard her heels clacking after me.

It was gratefully cool outside, compared with the Opera House, though probably still in the 80s here. I continued to walk rapidly and poor Anita must have had difficulty in keeping up, trotting along behind.

'Simon, wait,' she cried, plaintively, and as I was now, near the great crowded square, I relented and stopped to take her arm. I walked her more slowly but fairly steadily away from the mass of people weaving and dancing to their own samba bands.

'Where we go?' she asked, still plaintive.

'Away from all the people. I must have some rest from crowds and noise.'

She hurried along silently beside me for some time, as we turned more and more into the narrow by-ways, and further from the seething centre. Finally, the noise had faded completely and I stopped in the quiet street.

'Anita,' I said, 'it's nearly four o'clock. Let me take you home.'

'What is four? Is very early. Is still many hours today. Come on. We go back to dance.' And she Sambaed round me, clicking her fingers and humming the ever popular song of the season.

I was exasperated with her resistance. Drink had made her stubborn. 'Look, Anita, it was a wonderful ball, and I'm glad I took you, but I found it too hot and crowded and I've had enough. I want a little peace and quiet now. Let's go to your apartment and have a cup of coffee.'

She pouted. 'Is too early. We go later.'

'No,' I said firmly. 'We go now,' and I made to take her arm.

She snatched it away, stamping her foot: 'You Americanos all the same. Bed, bed, bed. I not go. No, no, no.' Her temperament had got the upper hand. She looked furious.

I was furious too. 'Well, don't then. There's a nasty word for girls like you in England. You've been leading me on with promises you did not intend to keep. Do what you like. I'm going home.' And I turned my back on her.

She flew at me then, suddenly enraged I suppose at my rejection – perhaps made aggressive with drink. Her hands clawed my face. The long red finger-nails caught the corner of my eye and tore down my cheek. I cannot

88

bear anyone going for my eyes. Instinctively, I lashed out and slapped her – hard. Behind that slap was the accummulation of my miserable frustrations, culminating in this incident now. She staggered back, dazed, and her high heels caught on the edge of the pavement. As she crashed down, she hit the side of her head on a low iron post. I don't know what it was. She lay still, her head at an odd angle, blood oozing from her temple.

Paralysed with horror, all my rage drained away. Was I a civilized man or a beast? Ruthless with girls unless I could get my own way? Was this another death on my hands? I took a fearful step forward to see if her heart was beating and, as I did so, my eye caught a movement at the end of the deserted street. It was no longer deserted. Standing rigidly staring, not very far from me, was the grey man.

This, I thought, is what he's been waiting for. He's been waiting for me to do just this, so that he can pin something on me. The thought flashed through my mind even as I turned and ran.

Panic was constricting my throat and I gasped and almost sobbed as I fled through the empty streets; the people around here were either asleep or in the centre of town, having a ball. I was sure I heard footsteps after me. My aim was to get back to the crowds and get lost in them, but my sense of direction was confused and I ran blindly down a turning which was an impasse; trapped! Then I saw a narrow passage through somebody's backyard, leading to another street. There was a gate barring my way and it took me a thousand years to negotiate it. When I came to the other side of the passage, I could see the bright lights of the carnival procession stands and hear the music once more.

Rushing headlong towards the noise, I came in at the

tail end of one of the professional 'schools'. About two to three hundred people, in various disguises, were preparing to go into the parade. My mind was working quickly and clearly now. I turned the mask from the back of my head and put it over my face. A stall nearby was selling carnival novelties. I bought three coloured paper garlands and draped them round my neck and a couple of sticks with streamers on them. There was a cordon round the actual school group to keep the public out, but as their Samba band struck up and they went into formation, I cried out, 'Pedro, Pedro,' as though late, and slipped under the cordon and under the eyes of the unsuspecting official guarding it. I tagged on, Sambaing and shaking my sticks with the streamers to the rhythm. No one could see who I was behind the mask and by now my Samba was passable. How long could I keep this up? My amateur status was bound to show through when I tired.

We must have been going for about ten minutes. It was strange being on the other side of the barrier, gyrating and waving at the roaring crowds in the stands. If I had not been keyed up to such a hysterical pitch, I might even have enjoyed the sensation. Carnival here is perhaps the last place on earth where the people discard all human cares and let themselves go in a kind of joyous abandon. I wished I could do the same. Instead, my nerves were snapping with tension. The problem now, having got into the procession, was how to get out again.

My next aim was to reach a plane and leave Rio as soon as possible. If the girl *was* dead, it could not be long before, with the help of the grey man, the police were on my track.

The wooden barriers on each side were high and my eyes searched feverishly for a break. At last I saw what I was looking for; a passage with an arrow pointing to

90

'WC'. It was on the opposite, left hand side, and I had to work my way rapidly over. One or two people spoke to me as I shook myself across their route. I said crazily, 'Olé – Vamos,' which was all the Spanish I could muster on the spur of the moment, and hoped it would pass for Portuguese. Members of the school stared while they continued to Samba and one said something angrily, but as I rushed into the WC passage, they must have come to the inevitable conclusion.

Once in the outer washroom, I tore off the paper garlands, and, removing my mask, dashed some cold water on my bleeding face. I stayed a couple of minutes to calm down, then put the mask on again and strolled out of the Exit on to the main road. Here I kept close into the crowds, moving always in the direction of the large square where I knew rows of taxis waited. As soon as it came into view, I snatched off the grinning mask and darted in and out of the crowds to the first taxi.

The driver wanted an exorbitant sum to take me back to my hotel. He could see I was anxious. Highway robbery – but I would have given him anything he asked to get me away. I had to control my impulse to direct him straight to the airport, so that I might take a plane anywhere, just so long as it was out of Rio. It was a panic notion. Rushing away without paying my bill and collecting my things would have created suspicion where none yet existed.

For the first time the fierce and erratic driving was not fast enough for me. I sat on the edge of my seat, willing him to hurry. The film chase was on – and I was in the thick of it.

The sea gleamed palely with the first light of dawn when I reached the hotel and paid off the taxi driver. The lobby had that bleak, early-morning look, the man at the desk sleepily working on his accounts.

I ran out again to the taxi before it moved off. 'Wait,' I called. 'How much do you want to take me to the airport?'

He named twice the correct amount.

I said, 'It's much too high, but I'll pay it, if you wait until I'm packed and ready to go.'

The driver grinned cheerfully. He'd landed a real sucker this time.

I hurried back to the man at the desk who was looking at me curiously now.

'What time is the first plane to England?' I asked him sharply. He went on staring at me with that wondering look and it was getting on my nerves. Then I saw myself in the big mirror behind him. I hardly recognized the face that glared back wildly. My hair was sticking out in all directions, blood had run down from the gash near the eye and sprayed out, clotting on my face. Below my chin dangled the grotesque mask which I had slung round my neck, giving me two diabolical faces instead of one.

I laughed, embarrassed, to reassure the desk clerk. 'Look,' I said, 'I've had quite a party at the Opera. I fell downstairs and cut myself. But I've had bad news from home; my mother's ill and I must go back to London at once.' I was talking too much. How could I have had bad news in the middle of an all-night Opera Ball?

The man had roused himself by now. 'Is not your hotel room booked for further nights?'

'Yes,' I said. 'Booked for two more nights and paid for in advance. Don't worry about that. I only have restaurant and bar bills. You must have a note of those. What about the plane?'

The man shrugged and shook his head. 'There's no plane to England until tomorrow evening and it may be impossible to get a seat.'

My stomach gave that sick jolt. 'Surely there is *some* plane to Europe before that?'

'Europe, yes. Lisbon, I think. I will have to find out.'

'Well, find out fast, there's a good chap, and book me on it – and make out my bill. I'm going upstairs now to clean up and pack. This is for your trouble.' I brought out a substantial dollar-note and pushed it across to him. I had decided to be peremptory rather than pleading. It worked.

His eyes lost their cold, considering look and became shut in and deferential. 'I will telephone the airline. I have a friend. He will try and get you on if he can. I think the plane leaves at seven thirty.'

'Splendid. That will do fine. I can pick up a connection to London from Lisbon quite easily.'

He bowed slightly. He was being paid handsomely to get me on that plane. That's where his problem ended. Mine certainly would not, but once out of the country, at least they would have a hard job pinning anything on me.

I went to my room, washed my face and it immediately looked less villainous. A nasty bruise was coming out under the eye. The scratch was quite long but not deep. It would heal in a few days. I threw my things together anyhow. After all, I was going home, even though it was via Lisbon.

By the time I came down, the man at the desk had my bill ready and my reservation made. I had to be at the airport to confirm and transfer my tickets as soon as possible, he said. In a few minutes I was in that taxi and on my hair-raising drive across town to my next escape hatch.

Delays on my South American flights were the pattern rather than the exception, so that I would have been surprised had the plane been on time. Nevertheless it was sheer agony, waiting hour after hour for this plane to take me off. I could not hide myself away as I had to be around to catch the latest bulletin on the delayed flight. I brought papers and hid behind them, reading the same meaningless lines over and over again, peering furtively around, fearful every minute that not only the grey man but a posse of Brazilian police would turn up to clap me into gaol. I was hot and the perspiration was rolling off me.

Finally, four hours later and half a stone lighter, I was marshalled through a door for searching. At first I resisted, thinking this was a sort of personal indictment which might lead to my arrest, but the official said, *'Securidad',* and I realized it was an anti hi-jack search. Everything was brought out: my dirty linen, the llama slippers I had bought for Mrs Hoggs, the silver mask.

It took nearly another hour searching all the passengers. Sick with nerves, my stomach was letting me down and I began to wonder whether I had picked up a bug. At last, we were allowed on to the plane. 'Please God, get me home out of this mess,' I prayed, without knowing to whom I was praying. Apart from accompanying my mother to church occasionally and making mechanical mumblings while my mind was on tennis or chess, I was not at all devout. But in times of stress, I still prayed like the small boy of long ago, trained to kneel by his bedside.

I fastened and unfastened my seat belt, ordered drinks, fell into an uneasy doze, was wakened with food – dozed again, ate again. The long hours of flying slipped by.

Now that I knew I was well on my way home, my senses, so intensely concentrated on the immediate necessity of escape, began to relax. The frozen barrier of fear that had numbed my brain was thawing, and the painful thoughts came back, hurting unendurably, like unhealed wounds.

It was always to Maria that my sorrowing mind returned. It was only with her that I was bound emotionally. Anita had been an artificial and disastrous adventure. All the same, if she were dead, I had killed her. Who would believe it was an accident? But let them prove it first. There were no witnesses other than the grey man. No one would associate me with her except he. It was his word against mine. Gingerly, I touched my bruised cheek, then sat up abruptly in my narrow plane seat. Of course, it was the wretched topaz ring which had acted as a knuckle duster. The jeweller – he would remember me! He could identify me as having bought the ring for Anita. It was a chilling thought and I cursed softly but violently: damn the acquisitive, go-getting little hell-cat; she deserved all she got. Perhaps not quite all, but I couldn't pretend to any tender feelings towards her, only shame at my own loss of control.

But Maria – that was different. She had trusted and loved me. What made it even more callous, was that I loved her. There was no excuse in her case. None whatever.

It was night now in the plane and the lights were dimmed. I could not read or sleep, only think, going over and over and over the events that had led to the present mess . . .

It's true that Kate Hetherington's Fête had been a financial success, but it nearly cost my mother her life. Rain came down in torrents at one stage and my mother's tent was soaked, so that though the sun came out again, it remained damp and steamy.

Mother stubbornly refused to go into the house; she claimed her tent was rigged out the way she wanted it and that too much time would be wasted setting it all up again. Her act was immensely popular and she had a long queue of clients. She went on telling fortunes until dusk, making a heap of tenpences for the Fête. The next day she had a heavy cold and after the long drive back home, it turned to pneumonia.

Three very anxious weeks followed. Had it not been for present-day drugs, my mother would not have recovered. Night and day nurses were engaged and, even so, Maria was run off her feet. She was a tower of strength during this period. There was no question of her coming to London on Tuesdays. My mother relied on her too much; in spite of the nurses, it was Maria she constantly called for. I would take as much time off as possible from the office to come down and stand in for her while she went for a walk or a rest. We did not make love – anxiety for my mother precluded that. At times, Maria would squeeze my hand sympathetically and I gave her an affectionate kiss, but that was all. My concern for my mother was paramount. It was a very worrying time.

After three weeks, Mother was out of danger and I could breathe more freely. She was now in considerable arthritic pain, however, and Maria still felt she should not absent herself for long. Anyway, she said she was too tired to make the trip to London at present. I did not press her, though I was now a little worried that she herself would crack up. She was looking thin and strained and had lost that wonderful glow of happiness that had surrounded her of late. In fact, she had become unusually abstracted and withdrawn. But I put it all down to the worry of my mother's illness.

96

Another month went by in this way. The night and day nurses were still in attendance as my mother, weak and in pain, needed a great deal of attention. However, she was getting steadily stronger and more like her old self, and I was beginning to feel the need of Maria again.

'Surely, darling, you could make an effort to come up next Tuesday,' I said to her at the week-end. 'These nurses are always under one's feet – it's an age since I've had you to myself. You need feeding up. Come on. You can name your own restaurant.'

She looked at me consideringly for a minute, as though words were trembling on the edge of her tongue. Then she changed her mind. Just nodding her head, she sighed wearily. 'OK. I'll come. I have to come up to London anyway.'

'What about?'

'Oh, I've some shopping and things to do,' she said a bit tersely, and turned away to her chores.

That Tuesday I put a bottle of champagne on ice while waiting for Maria. She would be round about seven she had said, repeating mysteriously that she had 'other things to do'. I felt we both needed a lift. The past weeks of intensive worry over mother had left their mark on me too. I had thought at one period that she would die, and the prospect of life without her seemed unendurable. She had for so long been my prop, I suppose; always comfortingly there, loving, never critical, anxious for my welfare.

Thinking about it now objectively, I realized that I had become spoilt. Yes, my darling mother with her cosseting love had made me too dependent on her emotionally. She had unwittingly drained some of my manhood from me. For too long I had used her as an excuse to shy away from the responsibilities and complications of marriage.

While waiting for Maria, however, anxiety for my mother still filled my mind. Her continued frailty worried me and I hoped that Maria would reassure and comfort me on that score. I was in the wrong mood, totally, for the shock that was to come.

It was Maria who needed comforting. She arrived late and I was getting restive and irritable. When she arrived she looked ill. She did not apologize. She had been to the doctor she said – again. It had been absolutely confirmed that she was to have a baby. The pregnancy was almost three months.

I was appalled and felt, as legions of men must have felt before me, trapped, and I panicked.

'Hell and damnation,' I said harshly. 'You must get rid of it.'

'I've done everything, but it hasn't worked. It was that day on the cliffs of Devon. I hadn't taken precautions. I tried to stop you but you wouldn't wait. Well, there we are. It's almost too late. It's nearly three months,' she repeated dully.

'We must do something and do it quickly,' I said, still brisk, insensitive to her distress. 'It couldn't have happened at a worse time. Mother must not get wind of this. Any upset might hold up her recovery.' How typical of me to fall back again on 'Mother', the ever ready excuse for my attitude.

'I suppose as a final resort I can have an abortion.' Maria's bleak look as she said this just pricked through my thick-skinned panic.

'Poor you. I'm afraid an abortion it will have to be,' I said grimly . . .

The lights in the plane flashed: 'Fasten your seat belts', and the hostess came round wakening people to warn them that there was turbulence ahead.

I stayed tensed up while the plane plunged and vibrated fiercely, so that one imagined the wings would drop off any minute. Not much fun flying in an electrical storm; anything can happen.

Then the pilot must have gone through it or above it and I became calmer. After all, I decided, if the end comes it will be quick and a release from my present anguish. But this sort of mood prevails only when one feels safe. The moment danger is present the instinct to survive predominates.

I dozed off and woke with an unhappy jolt when Maria's face swam before me as it had looked that evening: drawn, dark circles under her eyes. 'But, John,' she was pleading, 'it's our baby – *your* child – you want me to destroy.'

Unhinged, no doubt, by the strain of the past weeks, topped by this crisis, I said a brutal, unforgivable thing. 'I don't *want* a child and I trusted you not to land us in this mess. After all, you'd had plenty of experience before I met you.'

In one movement, Maria rose from the armchair where she had been sitting, collected her bag and coat from a nearby chair, and stood a moment, trembling. Her face looked ghastly.

'It's your mother,' she said in a low, passionate voice. 'You are are so obsessed with her, there is no room left in your heart to love anyone else. I thought you loved me, in spite of yourself. I see now I was wrong – again! You are as cruel as the other. I'm a fool.' She started towards the door.

'Maria, wait. I'm sorry. It was a beastly thing to say. I

99

didn't mean it. Where are you going? What are you going to do?'

Maria stopped and faced me. 'Kill myself. It would be simpler. I'm tired of living.' Her low voice was more chilling than a dramatic declamation. Her eyes, unseeing, were focused on an inner vision. She turned again.

'Don't be silly, Maria. We are not in a Victorian melodrama. You must let me give you some money. Look, I've three hundred pounds in cash in the flat. You can take it right away and do this thing safely and quickly. No one will know.'

I had been following her into the hall and talking to her back as she continued towards the front door. Now she stopped again. Her slim figure seemed taller; the green eyes had clouded to the colour of an angry sea. She looked at me with hauteur, disgust, pain and hatred.

'Stuff your silly money,' she said. 'Do you really think I would take money from a murderer!' And then, she did a shocking thing: she spat on my carpet and went out, shutting the door hard behind her.

I was furiously upset. Filthy, foreign habits, I raged. My mother is right. No English girl would behave this way.

In spite of my stunned distress, or perhaps because of it, I went into the kitchen to fetch a cloth and washed out the spot. It is a precious Chinese rug in light colours, and spittle can stain . . .

The remorse had come later. I went to bed disturbed and enraged and woke up still disturbed, but now horrified at the enormity of my callousness.

The Law Courts kept me busy all morning, and when I found time to telephone Maria in the afternoon the nurse said she was out.

'When will she be back?' I asked.

'I'm afraid I don't know.' The nurse's voice sounded hesitant.

Just then my secretary came in to announce a client.

'Please tell her to call me when she comes in,' I said hurriedly, and rang off.

I waited irritably for her call all the afternoon, finding it hard to concentrate on my work. Then, with increasing unease, sat through the evening in my flat, hoping the phone would ring. It did not.

I would not telephone again. My mother always heard the bell and became curious. It was easier for Maria to call me. Then, as the evening wore on, I started a letter, but tore it up. Tomorrow was Thursday. If I posted it in the morning, I would arrive in person on the Friday, before my letter. Better to think over what to say when I saw her at the week-end. I sat and thought until my brain was buzzing. By the time I drove down on Friday afternoon I was full of half-baked ideas which I intended to put to her for discussion.

Manipulating the Porsche through the country lanes, I talked to myself, rehearsing the different things I might say.

'Maria, I'm sorry. But you do see that it would be too much of a shock for Mother in her present weak state. You must let me help you to get rid of it safely. Please.' Or:

'I'll help you financially to have the baby if you don't want an abortion, and you could get it adopted. People are screaming for babies, I'm told.'

Too cowardly to face up to the obvious solution – tell my mother everything and marry Maria, I yet wanted desperately to arrive at *some* understanding with her. For I loved Maria, however ignobly I had reacted to her news.

The front door was opened by a tall, rather hefty blond girl. It was not the day nurse.

'Hallo. Who are *you*?' I asked, surprised.

'I'm the new temporary. You must be Mrs Devigne's son,' she said. 'She's expecting you. Excuse me, I'm beating up some supper.' She was the breezy type again.

My mother was sitting in her chair in the darkened sitting-room.

'Where's Maria?' I barked at her. 'And why are you sitting in the dark?'

'Maria's gone. And my hands are hurting too much to wheel the chair over to the light switch.'

'Gone? When? Where?'

'She left on Thursday. She said she was ill and wanted time off. So I suggested she went back to her parents in Greece, who could look after her. I gave her three months' salary and her fare, so she'll be all right.'

My mother knew. Of course. She had paid the compensation Maria would not take from me. How dare she deal with my problmes in this high-handed manner! I was choking with rage and frustration, clenching my fists to control myself. Angry words boiled inside me. Yet Mother, sitting in her chair in the gloomy room, seemed so pathetic, I merely snapped on the light. 'What's this new thing about your hands?' I asked harshly.

'They've started hurting more and more these past weeks. I can't work on my embroidery now. Could you get me my pain-killing pills? The nurse is out and the new girl doesn't know where anything is.' She sighed resignedly.

God, I thought, if her embroidery goes, then her sight so that she can't look at telly, what will be left to her? Except me. There's always me. My anxiety for her overcame my anger. I went to fetch the pills.

The habit of worrying and assuming responsibility for my mother triumphed. I called the doctor on Saturday and he gave her some new drugs. There was little else he could do. I went through the boring routine of showing the present girl everything. I could hardly be civil.

I could also hardly wait to get back to London to think out what best to do about tracking down Maria, and I left on the Sunday afternoon. I wanted to get in touch with a Mrs Stephens, who had found Maria for us. She had not come through the Agency.

She was at home when I telephoned.

'Mrs Stephens,' I said, 'the girl Maria you sent us has left rather suddenly and my mother did not take her address. Do you know where I might find her? I have some things of hers I want to return.'

'Oh, I *am* sorry. I hope there's no trouble. She seemed so good with the Plummers' children.'

'No. No trouble. She left for personal reasons. Can you help me?'

'I'm afraid not. I have no idea whatever. Of course, the Plummers may have her address.'

'Oh, then perhaps you would kindly tell me where to contact the Plummers?'

'Well, he was posted to Mexico City. I believe they are there now.'

'Mexico City?'

I must have sounded dismayed because she added hurriedly: 'If you write c/o the Embassy there, it's bound to find them. Sorry I can't be more helpful.'

I thanked her and put the receiver down in despair. By the time I had written to Mexico and they had answered, even if they knew where Maria was, which seemed unlikely, it would be too late. She would have acted for better or worse. She would be gone; to Greece, perhaps, with the baby though, knowing Maria, I doubted this very much. She would not want to distress her parents. Rather than that, she might well follow her first impulse and put an end to her life. I was scared. There were no mutual friends I could contact as we had always kept strictly to ourselves – my wish rather than hers. If she were still in London, how to find her? I shrank from going to the police and having them pry into my private affairs.

Clutching at straws, I persuaded myself that she would forgive me and contact me again after all. She was intelligent. Surely she would understand that it was my long repressed jealousy of her previous lover which had burst through in that brutal attack. Surely she would realize this, and know that by now I was miserably ashamed.

All week I lived in the hope of that possibility. Every time the telephone rang, I snatched at it anxiously. The disappointment was greater with each false alarm. After a few days, my hopes faded. Why should she call me? She had every right to despise and hate me, even supposing she was still around.

I was deeply worried and, to add to my gloom, my mother now showed signs of a relapse. The day nurse rang to say she was running a low temperature, and should she call the doctor.

'Of course, immediately,' I said. 'Let me know what he says. I'll come any time if necessary, otherwise I'll be down on Friday.' I sighed as I put down the receiver. Maria would have called the doctor automatically. She had quietly run the household during my mother's illness and they missed her guiding hand.

When I arrived on the Friday, I found my mother obviously still suffering from some sort of mental disturbance. She was fretful and frail; her eyes had a worried look. I realized then that the sudden loss of Maria was a shock. She had grown to depend on her and it occurred to me for the first time that she was fond of her, too. What a mess, I thought: my mother trying to protect me and I, my mother, and Maria made the victim of this misdirected concern.

I tentatively broached the subject of Maria as Mother and I ate a solitary dinner. The temporary help and the nurse had gone together to the village cinema at my suggestion. They got on my nerves. It was peaceful without them.

'Mother,' I said, 'Maria surely gave you some indication of where she would be. Have you her home address in Crete?'

My mother looked troubled and stopped eating abruptly.

'No,' she said. 'Maria and I had little to say to each other at the end. Once it was understood she was leaving, I made out a cheque and she disappeared for the day on the Wednesday. I know she cashed the cheque but she had not said positively whether she would be returning to Greece. She came back late, packed, and left early on Thursday morning while I was still asleep. It was she who had arranged with the Agency to send the temporary girl that day. She left no address. No clue where she was going.' Mother pushed her plate of food away. 'I've had enough,' she said. It was an indication of her very real distress, to refuse a favourite dish. My mother was fond of her food.

The question had had to be asked, but there was no point in upsetting her any further. After that, the subject was closed between us.

The new girl took Saturday and most of Sunday as her

time off. I had arranged this with her. Seeing her around was like salt in my wound, underlining the loss of Maria. It made me irritable towards her. The day nurse, a strong, sensible woman, and I could cope quite well between us.

Mrs Hoggs came in on Saturday morning to do the cleaning. I tackled her at the first opportunity. 'Hugs darling,' I said (she had known me since I was a small boy), 'did you see Maria before she left? Did she tell you where she was going?' I knew they had got on well together.

'It came as a real shock to me, Mister John. On Wednesday I thought she looked poorly, but she didn't say anything, and on Thursday, by the time I came in, she had gone. Just like that. I couldn't believe it. She did leave me a note. Here it is.' She produced a folded piece of paper from her apron pocket.

I read: '*Good-bye, Mrs Hoggs. I'm so sorry not to have seen you before leaving, particularly as you've always been so sweet to me and such a wonderful help during these past difficult weeks. Look after youself and don't work too hard. It's not worth beating yourself up for anybody. Please dispose of the things I've left behind – I won't be needing them any more. Love, Maria.*'

It was written on a plain piece of paper. The note of bitterness in the penultimate sentence was the only indication of her fellings.

Mrs Hoggs said, 'She was the nicest person we ever had here. She was real nice to me. I shall miss her.' She wiped away a tear. 'Perhaps there was trouble in her family. I asked your mother but she went all up in the air, so I shut up. I didn't want to upset her, you see.'

'Did Maria leave much behind?' I asked.

'Yes. Lots of things.'

'What sort of things?'

'Well, books and clothes. Her boots now, nearly new they were, and fitted me lovely, so I kept them; but the rest, well, I asked your mother and she said: take them to Oxfam. No, they was all too small for me, she being so slim, you see. But I know she wanted me to have something of hers, so I took the boots. I don't know why she went so sudden and left her things.'

I gave her a hug. 'It was a shock to us all, her sudden departure. I know she was fond of you, and I wondered whether she had confided in you.'

'No. But she was very fond of you, too, Mister John. I could tell.' I met her eyes. There was no reproach in them, only sympathy.

I turned away, near to tears myself. 'Well, if she writes and gives you an address, promise to let me know. I'd like to get in touch with her.' Hollow words. I knew Maria would never write. The conviction was steadily growing in me that she was dead.

Later that day, passing Maria's bedroom, on impulse I went inside. I had often been in there secretly when overwhelmed by the need to kiss her and hold her in my arms for a short while. It was amazing how stripped of her personality the room had become. The new girl slept there now and though the furnishings were the same, everything else was so different, it was like walking into a totally strange place. The photographs of Maria's young mother and baby sister, taken years ago, and her handsome Cretan father with the wide eyes rather like Maria's, had been replaced by pop stars in gaudy frames. Clothes littered the floor and bed and the smell of the toilet water used by this girl was sickly in my nostrils. The spilt powder on the dressing table was almost a shock. Maria never used powder.

There was no clue here of Maria's last feverish moments of probable despair. Mrs Hoggs had cleared away anything left in the waste-paper basket. I had hoped, faintly, maybe to find a scribbled note screwed up. I walked over to the window and looked through at the view she must have gazed at for the last time. It was November. There had been a storm and the autumn leaves lay black and sodden on the ground. The bare branches of the trees were bleak against a grey sky. I shivered. Where was Maria? I felt as cold and desolate as those trees.

I tried to put myself in her tussled thoughts; should she go home to her parents? No, it would only bring them unhappiness. Village life in Crete was not likely to look with favour on an illegitimate child. More likely, feeling nothing but bitterness, she would think it pointless to go on. She had known anguish before, but never like this.

She had said of the things she left behind: 'I won't be needing them any more.' The sentence held for me a sinister confirmation of my fears. Knowing her consideration for others, I doubted she would do anything messy, like cutting her wrists, or putting her head in a gas oven. When in France, I had shown her the spot where Corbusier had drowned whilst out swimming.

'A good death,' Maria had said quietly. 'The sea is kind to those who love her. She would take them gently into her arms.'

Maria loved the sea. Looking at the stormy sky now, I formed a clear picture of her swimming out to sea, her black hair streaming around her. She had a strong will, and once her mind was made up, she would follow her decision through.

Then my thoughts jumped ahead in a vivid flash: I saw her beautiful body mutilated, eaten by fishes, the eyes

108

glazed, the face bloated. I turned away from the window, sickened.

The image had been so overwhelming, that from then on I could only think of Maria as drowned.

The days passed. I scanned the newspapers for possible reports of a recovered body. I found nothing. But the conviction of her death grew in me and took me over. It was after that that the burden of guilt, remorse and loneliness began to weigh on me. I started having these desolate sea nightmares. Sometimes the subliminal image of Maria, drowned and mutilated, jumped before my inner eye and I would wake crying out, almost sobbing in my half sleep. The words: 'I won't be needing them any more', echoed in my mind.

I became more and more silent, immersed in my own miserable thoughts. I went off my games; at squash I was listless, at chess hopeless. Worst of all, of course, it told on my work, until finally Edward took a hand and banished me to foreign travel in the hope of curing me of my sickness. I had agreed, thinking it would give me the opportunity to contact the Plummers.

And what good had it done me? I speculated now, sitting in the plane on my way home. It had profited me not at all. I had gone to South America to escape my conscience and found it chasing me everywhere. The dark shadow of anxiety brooded over all the places and people I had seen. Far from rational, my tensions had finally led me to behave like a fool again. I sighed, realizing that nothing in life can be appreciated if one's inner peace is disturbed.

The sky was brightening rapidly and the dawn light hurt my eyes. They ached and I closed them and must have fallen asleep. The stewardess woke me some hours later; we were about to touch down in Lisbon.

CHAPTER ELEVEN

Even though I had never been to Lisbon before, I felt immediately at home there. It was Europe. I could have kissed the ground.

As soon as I booked into a hotel, my first need after the long hours of flying was for a hot soak to take the ache out of my cramped limbs. I peered anxiously into the bathroom mirror. The hollow-eyed face with a livid scratch down one side which stared back did nothing to reassure me. I decided to stay a day in Lisbon to rest. Tomorrow would be Friday and nearer to the time I was expected home.

My next need was for a chemist. I spoke no Portuguese, but with English you can get by practically the world over. The pharmacist was helpful: he cleaned the cut and put some stuff on it, then covered the worst with sticking plaster. I went out of his shop looking less of a villain and more like a wounded soldier.

A travel agent next, to book my plane for tomorrow, and then a cable to my mother, telling her of my arrival.

This done, I strolled around the lovely old town. I noticed, vaguely, tall buildings in pastel shades with coloured tiles shining on the outside. I took in my surroundings very superficially, my mind being too much under stress from the events of – was it yesterday? The humming activity around me was comforting, but my brain still seethed with its many problems. Would the grey man have informed the police? Was Anita dead? If she had recovered consciousness, the name and address I had given her were false. But the grey man *must* know my identity. And then their was the jeweller. They would soon break through the camouflage. I found myself beating my head with my clenched fist, impotently. If Anita were dead, they would certainly be after me; if alive and badly hurt, she could still indict against me.

I stopped my purposeless walking; I had been tearing along the narrow, crowded streets, blind to everything, my movements matching my agitated thoughts. I went into a bar and had two whiskies. I felt calmer and realized that I was hungry.

The open air café where I sat for lunch was in a large, sunny square busy with traffic and people. After the torrid heat of Rio, the air was refreshingly cool and sparkled like the wine I was now drinking. I took a deep breath; I felt safe here. Should I go to ground in Lisbon for a while? No one would know I'm here, I thought wildly. Then I remembered I had just sent my mother a cable. Anyway, I couldn't keep on the run for ever. I must go home now, and if the worst happened I would be better equipped to face it there.

My leisurely lunch, followed by a liqueur and coffee, made me considerably more relaxed. I decided to walk again, calmly, not in a state of panic.

This place was full of Anitas: dark, slight girls, with flashing eyes and good teeth. They moved me not at all. I wondered at myself for having made a pass at Anita. I had not truly desired her. My love for Maria had become so obsessive, it had dimmed my lust for other women. My real need had been to get away from the grey man and the

111

noise. The urgency of my demands had been, not for Anita's body, but the privacy of her apartment with her presence there to comfort me. It had been such an utterly futile quarrel; a futile waste of her life – and my own freedom. Because, though I moved freely still, I was already imprisoned in my mind. My guilt had now deepened into the uneasy certitude that I was a callous destroyer.

Lisbon was built on a series of hills. Some of the long, straight streets had vistas of mountains at the end, some led down to the blue sea. I took one to the sea. It always attracted me, too. Maria and I had had that, as so many other things, in common. My physical ache for her, temporarily numbed, was returning; travel seemed merely to have emphasized my loneliness, my loss.

Deep misery overflowed again as I stood gazing out to sea and I felt a strong urge to jump in and rejoin my mermaid. I remember saying to Maria once when she flashed out from under the water to swim beside me: 'Hallo, mermaid. You look just like one, with your green eyes and long, wet hair.'

'But I've no tail,' she had laughed. *'Vive la différence.'*

May be she had a tail now.

I shook off my morbid fancies. It was time to go home. At least my mother would be glad to see me again and so would Edward and Rosemary and those of my clients who relied on me. Clutching tight to these crumbs of comfort, I walked back slowly through the soft sunset, watching the surrounding hills turn pink and the tiles on the tall houses glow in the evening light.

I had come to the conclusion that this was a most rewarding town architecturally. So much of it still stood unchanged since the 18th century when it had been rebuilt after a devastating earthquake, so that the houses

112

uniformly reflected the elegance of that period. I had seen no shanty towns, no ugly skyscrapers. It seemed inviolable.

Soothed by its beauty, and tired out by my physical and mental wanderings, that night I fell, unjustly perhaps, into the soundest of sleeps.

BOOK TWO

RETURN

CHAPTER TWELVE

My mother was waiting for me in her best bib and tucker. The dark lines of pain on her face had faded a lot and her eyes held the old sparkle.

'You look marvellous, darling,' I said. 'It's so good to be home.'

She held me a while after hugging me and gave a puzzled frown. 'I wish I could say the same for you, my child. You look thin, and what's that horrid scratch on your face?'

'A tarantula got me,' I said jokily. 'It's nothing. Rio was wild in the carnival. I think I picked up a bug, that's why I'm thin – but I'm all right.'

'You must see a doctor at once,' my mother said briskly. 'Never let these things get a hold. Look,' she added, going straight into her own excitements as was her way, 'Kate's back and she keeps sending me plants to make up for catching flu at the fête. She was horrified when she found out but now, as always, she's overdoing it. There's enough here to stock two gardens our size. I wish she'd stop. Perhaps you can explain that it will give you too much work planting it out. She's sent three varieties of camellias and six bushes of azaleas. We'll have to re-plan the garden – and get in some peat.'

So she went on for some time. Kate Hetherington had not known before of my mother's illness. She had left almost immediately after the fête for Kenya, to stay with one of her sons. I had not written about it, unwilling to upset her. Now, it seemed, she was back and, in character, her gesture of sympathy was larger than life. My mother was right; there were pots all over the terrace, standing as they had been delivered, waiting for my attention.

'So you've work right through the spring into summer,' my mother was saying. 'Fortunately, being in pots, they can wait for ages. It must have cost a fortune.'

'Don't worry, Mums,' I said. 'We'll have fun planning a new garden together at week-ends. But I'll tell Kate to stop. Enough is enough. Have you any other news?'

'What sort of news?' my mother said sharply. She so often read my mind. I had been thinking of Maria – but also, vaguely, of the grey man. Sooner or later, I knew, he would make contact. 'Well, yes,' Mother went on, 'I got rid of the woman who was here when you left. She got on my nerves, always repeating everything as though I were deaf or daft. I've a good girl now. She's no beauty, but jolly – and she's strong. I told her to go out tonight as I wanted you to myself.'

I wondered what 'no beauty' covered. My mother had said it with a twinkle. Was she playing safe? The nurses had left long ago. Mother no longer needed them. She was back on form.

'No beauty' appeared next morning and I saw what it was all about. I admire coloured girls if they are beautiful; many have the most gorgeous figures and a tremendous sexuality. This poor woman had the worst of both worlds. Coarse features, a mottled skin and a massive thick body. She looked strong all right. She could have lifted Mother with one hand and me with the other. Still, she was jolly and laughed a lot, showing healthy, even teeth. They were her best feature.

It turned out that she had done a lot of nursing and was

an excellent cook. So Mother had chosen well, after all. Her name was Daisy, and very soon we became friends. I found her fun and didn't notice her looks after a while. She must have been in her forties and had come from Jamaica some twenty years ago.

'Daisy, Daisy, give me your answer, do,' I chanted, when I wanted something done.

'John, John, get you gone. You haven't put your trousers on,' she would reply, and we both laughed like children. No wonder Mother looked well. Daisy was a life-giving force. She helped more than anyone to bring back a feeling of normality to me too, in spite of the nightmare quality of my present existence.

We had a cheerful week-end. My mother was delighted with her Mexican chain and the jewel I had bought in Rio; on impulse, I gave Daisy a silver bracelet I had picked up for my secretary. She was thrilled. I don't suppose she was often given pretty things. My secretary had plenty of bracelets. An expensive bottle of scent would doubtless please her more.

Daisy cooked a delicious lunch on Sunday and made my favourite blueberry pie.

'Eat up, eat up,' she said, piling my plate with a second helping. 'When I first saw you, I thought: here comes the ghost of Gregory Peck. I never believed you were flesh and blood at all, at all.'

I laughed. 'Travel makes you thin, Daisy.'

'Boy, you sure must have travelled,' she said. 'Time you stayed home and fattened up a bit.'

'If you stick around a while, it looks like I'll soon do just that.'

'Oh, I'll stick around all right. You won't get rid of me that easy.' She gave my mother a wink. 'When I like a place, I stick. Not much of the temporary about me.'

I saw that my mother was taking it all in good part. It

118

seemed like a happy alliance, at last.

I telephoned Edward to say I was back.

'Am I glad to hear your voice,' he said. 'Robinson's made a mess of his company books and the Tax office is out for blood. I've had to get Counsel's opinion. I've called a meeting for eleven tomorrow. Can you be there?'

'I'll be there,' I said. Robinson was my client. He was a property developer and his account the biggest we handled.

By Monday I was feeling much better. Even the scratch was healing and had lost its angry glare. The bruise under the eye had faded, so that when I met Edward in the morning, I was no longer looking such a mess.

He gave me a quick glance. 'You don't seem any fatter. Had a good time? How are you feeling?'

'Fine, just fine,' I answered automatically.

'Good.' Edward was crisp. 'All hell's been let loose here since you left. I've just time to brief you before the meeting. Let's go into my room. I've all the papers there.'

He was harassed, poor chap. Shouldering the load of my own clients as well as his for three weeks was all right provided things did not go seriously wrong. I looked forward to taking over my share again. I needed to have my mind fully occupied.

'How's Rosemary?' I asked, as we sat down.

'As well as can be expected.' Edward shrugged. 'She's always sick the first three months.'

'No! Not another?' I said, startled.

'Oh, you didn't know before you left, of course. It hadn't been confirmed. Well, if it's a boy, it'll make two all.' I could see that he was pleased. 'By the way, before we start, she wants you to come to dinner one evening. She's dying to hear about your travels. We both are.

119

When can you come?'

'Wednesday?'

'The sooner the better. I know it's all right. We've no dates as Johnnie's recovering from measles. Rosie never goes out when the kids are sick.'

'Good. I look forward to it. I've a few things for you all.'

'That's on then. Now, to work.' We quickly became immersed in the intricate problems of our tricky case. It went that way all day.

My flat was quietly waiting for me in the evening. The cleaner had been in regularly, so that it was cared for and polished – but there was more to it than that. An air of expectancy, or was it a presence? I sensed. It was so strong a feeling, that I even went into the bedroom and flicked on the light to make sure no one was there. I was not frightened – just uneasy. Was it Maria? Had she moved in gently to haunt me? Or was it just my loneliness, picturing her moving around in the intimacy of our Tuesdays together.

I could see her now, coming out of the bedroom into the bathroom, out of the bathroom into the kitchen, barefoot, with very little on. I would sit with a whisky in my hand, doting on her body, watching its curves as she bent and stretched and fetched and carried. 'Come on, lazybones, lend a hand,' she would cry. 'Coming,' I'd say and go into the kitchen to kiss her hungrily, and sometimes we would forget what we were cooking and return to the bedroom again.

I took the cases into my room now and unpacked. Carefully wrapped at the bottom, was the mask. Not only did it remind me of Maria, but it was a beautiful piece of craftsmanship. It would have a place of honour on my walls. I gazed at it. hopelessly.

'Darling,' I whispered, 'why did I let you go? I love

you so much. Why, why, has it gone so wrong?' Then for the first time since Maria's disappearance, I broke down and cried bitterly. The accumulated tensions and miseries of the past weeks had finally overwhelmed me.

The days were not too bad. They were so packed with work I had no time for other thoughts. My secretary organized coffee and sandwiches and I plodded through my lunch hour. By the end of the day on Tuesday, I had spoken with most of my more pressing clients and reassured them that I was back attending to their affairs.

It was in the evening, sitting alone in my flat, that my own worries crowded in on me again. Where was the grey man? I wished I knew what part he played. At times I had thought him just an imagined menace, conjured up by my guilty conscience, but he had become an extremely tangible one in that he had witnessed Anita's accident. What did he intend doing about that? What sort of a cat and mouse game was he playing?

The telephone rang stridently and I jumped. I wasn't expecting a call and I hesitated before picking it up. Mother never phoned – she saved all news for the weekend. Still, it might be Rosemary.

I picked up the receiver, saying nothing, just listening. 'Hallo,' said a male voice.

Quietly, I replaced the receiver. I didn't know the voice. The hair on the back of my neck prickled. Was it a wrong number? Or the grey man, at last? My clients never rang at home. I was ex-directory for that reason.

The telephone was silent – for an hour. I had settled down with the back log of my correspondence, mostly bills and circulars, when its urgent clamour broke out once more. This time I didn't pick it up. Going into my bedroom, I closed the door firmly and let it ring in the empty room.

I was glad to be dining out at Edward's tomorrow night.

Rosemary gave me a warm kiss next evening and said, 'Lovely to see you back, John. What have you done to your face? One of those South American wild cats got you?'

'Wilder than that. Grr!' I joked and changed the subject swiftly. 'What have *you* been up to? The milkman again? Or is it the young god from the supermarket this time?'

It was the family joke. Edward refuted the children; they were all too blond and beautiful to be his, he claimed.

'I'm a reformed character. This one's a boy and he's going to be tough, dark and long-suffering – just like Edward. Even *he* will have to admit paternity.' Rosemary always bloomed in pregnancy. She looked happy. The pill did not suit her, but having children did.

'Where are they all?' I asked, looking round. 'I've some presents for them.'

'The mice are in their cots.' Rosemary always referred to her brood as 'mice'; it was her definition for 'the patter of tiny feet'. 'Johny's getting over measles, but the girls will be allowed to come down and say hallo. Later, though, when you've had a drink.'

'Now,' Rosemary said, handing me my drink and sitting comfortably. 'Shoot.'

I started a thumbnail sketch of my travels in Mexico. 'Look, Rosemary,' I said, producing the fob I had bought her, 'I got this in the Indian market outside Mexico City.' As I said it, I had a vivid picture of the grey man staring down at me from the gallery above. The sounds around me faded, and though Rosemary was talking, I didn't hear a word she said.

She repeated, 'Was it, John?'

'Was it what?' I asked, coming to.

'Made by an Indian? It's so sophisticated in design.'

'Yes. They are gifted craftsmen,' and I went on to talk about Taxco and the silver workshops there. The picture of the grey man, in the square this time, intruded on my thoughts and I fell silent.

Rosemary broke in, 'It all sounds a bit lonely. Didn't you make any friends?'

'I did, as a matter of fact. A group of Americans in Mexico. We went about together quite a lot.' I described the wonders of Acapulco and the perilous divers. 'Peru was quite different,' I continued, and went into a eulogy on the sweeping grandeur of the Andes and the charm of the Peruvian Indians. When I came to Machu Picchu, I stopped dead and a tremor went through me. The grey man was there again, staring into my camera.

'You don't seem to have liked it.' Rosemary was puzzled.

'It was grim,' I said and drained my drink.

Edward rose quickly. 'Have another, to wash the memory away. Let the poor man have a drink in peace, Rosie. You ask too many questions.' Edward was sensitive in his reactions.

'But Rio,' Rosemary insisted. 'That must have been a livelier scene than all those gloomy mountains. Didn't you chat up any pretty girls there? Was it fun?'

'It was explosive,' I said. 'Full of lovely girls. Anita—' I stopped, horrified. 'Well, she was one of a crowd I met one night. They were all swallowed up by the carnival,' I ended lamely, furious with myself.

Little Helena and Jane came to my rescue by appearing at that precise moment. 'Please, Mummy, you said we could come down to see Uncle John.' They looked like a couple of angels in long white nighties, their shining pale gold hair flowing around them.

'Just five minutes,' Rosemary said. 'While I go and see to dinner.'

'Uncle John' – Helena, aged seven, was full of womanly guile – 'Mummy says if I ask if you bwought me a present, I can't have it – so I won't ask.'

Jane, aged only five, said, 'I want a dlink, please.' And proceeded to sip some of her father's whisky.

I produced the charm bracelets and the little girls skipped about in delight, trying them round their necks, their ankles, their arms, and each other.

'While I'm about it, here's yours,' I said, presenting Edward with his cuff links.

He unwrapped the black tissue paper and snapped open the box. He gave a low whistle. 'I've never had anything like this before. I shall have to get a suit to go with them.' He peered at the inside of the lid and read out the name of the jeweller: 'Copacabana, Rio de Janeiro,' he concluded. 'Sounds very, very swanky.'

I felt myself go red. What a stupid fool I am, I thought, just dropping the clues around. I could never make a successful criminal. Of course I should have taken the cuff links out of the box so as not to associate myself with Anita's jeweller. Too late now.

Rosemary was back. 'Chop, chop,' she was saying. 'Come along.' And after a lot of hugging and kissing, the children were bundled upstairs.

Rosemary had cooked a gorgeous meal; she was a gorgeous girl. How lucky Edward was, I brooded, as I delved into my game pie. My own gorgeous girl could have produced such a meal and they might have been sitting at table with us, in our flat – our home. Suddenly, I was no longer hungry and had to force myself to eat out of politeness.

'Don't finish it if it's too much,' Rosemary said tactfully. 'I want you to leave some room for my special pud

You are sweet to have bought us such lovely things. We're all thrilled,' she went on. 'Now, if you've got the strength, tell us some more about the carnival. Is it worth a special trip to Rio?'

I felt a great distaste, a terrible disinclination to talk about it. But I braced myself.

'First of all, it was terribly hot, going up as far as one hundred and ten degrees in the day. Then a lot of the people are stoned throughout the carnival period, I gather. But if you can one day, go and see it. A madness takes the people – it is a unique spectacle. Once you're there, though, don't pick holes; you must let yourself go along with it. Otherwise you may not be able to bear it.'

'You sound sad about it,' Rosemary mused. 'In fact, I don't believe you enjoyed any of your travels much.'

'Not much,' I said in a burst of frankness. 'I'm glad to be home.' Yet 'glad' was not the right word. It had a false ring. Comforted, by Mother and friends, yes; but gladness was gone.

In the silence that followed my remark, I saw Edward and Rosemary look at each other. Rosemary got up to clear the plates and gave me a light kiss on the forehead.

'Dear John, you've become so serious. You, who were the terror of the tennis club. I rang you last night, but there was no reply. I hoped it meant you were out with some girl again.' She knew about Tuesdays.

I shook my head. 'No. No girl. When did you ring?'

'Oh, I don't know – about nine.'

So the second call had been Rosemary. 'I must have slipped out to buy some cigarettes,' I lied.

'Cigarettes?' Rosemary was shocked. 'But you gave them up ages ago.'

'Well, I'm smoking again. Not much.' That, at least, was true.

'Here am I, trying to break Edward of the filthy habit

and offering you as a shining example! Don't light up, please, until you've tasted the raspberry mousse.'

Watching Rosemary disappear into the kitchen, I was amused to think that she was actually concerned about my present lack of interest in women. Since having an affair with one of her friends some years ago, which had ended rather badly, she had looked upon me as a hopeless roué and refused to introduce me to any others.

'I'm not going to procure for you,' she had said. 'You are quite able to find any amount of girls, ready to throw themselves at your feet, on your own initiative.'

'You make me sound like a Pasha with a harem. Lying around, watching my women come and go, idly flicking the whip from time to time.'

Rosemary had shrugged. 'Wouldn't know about the whip; some may enjoy it. It's the icy lash of your indifference they can't stand.'

After that we had never discussed my love life again. For her to feel concern for me on this score now, I must present a pretty sorry picture in her eyes.

About eleven o'clock I rose to go. 'Thank you, Rosemary, for a delicious meal,' I said, kissing her. 'It's great seeing you all again. By the way, how's my boy?' That was John, my three-year-old godson.

'He'll be all right in a day or two. He's very upset to have missed you. Why don't you come to dinner again next week, then you'll see him?'

'I'd love to. Look,' I said, producing the grinning carnival mask out of my overcoat pocket, 'I brought this along for him. Do you think it's too grim?'

'It's utterly ghoulish, but I expect he'll love it. That will cheer him up.'

Afterwards, thinking about it in bed, I felt uneasy at having passed that mask on to little Johny. I had washed the blood carefully from the inside, but that had not exorcised it, in my view, from its evil associations. I wished now that I had simply destroyed it.

The next evening, Thursday, I decided to spend at my flat, cleaning my more precious possessions, those that the daily was not allowed to touch. The telephone rang. Rosemary? Putting down my rags and brushes, I picked it up.

It was the unknown male voice again saying the single word, 'Hallo!'

I put the receiver down quickly and angrily. What the hell was he playing at? Trying to frighten me, leading to blackmail perhaps? That was the new thought seeping into my mind. Maybe he hadn't said anything to the police, hoping to squeeze me. Well, he was going to get a run for his money. I wouldn't answer the phone again. He would have to confront me face to face. For the first time the possibility of removing this man from my life came into my head. How easy it is to think in terms of murder when up against it, I thought. Babe had been right when she said we all had the killer instinct. At any rate the intention is there, though one may jib at the act. I wished with all my heart that the grey man would drop dead.

The telephone rang again. I looked at it as thought it were a snake hissing. Snatching up my coat and scarf, I went down to the Porsche.

As soon as I got her on to the motorway I let her go. It was terrific to have her in my hands again, sharing the death wish. Although I did not want to die. I am a tidy man, and the bewildering tangle of loose ends surrounding me needed sorting out.

Tomorrow I was going to my mother's as usual, to work on the garden and comfort her with my presence. Now, however, pleasing her and looking after my clients seemed no longer a sufficient justification for my existence. In fact, I had come to question all my previous values: had I not been so devoted, my mother might have married again and led a more amusing life; as for my clients, some other solicitor could certainly have dealt with them as adequately as I.

So, my life had lost its purpose and the only way to go on living, I told myself grimly, was to find the key again. At present my thoughts floundered in a maze – dark avenues of guilt and fear that led to nowhere. The grey man had yet to play out his rôle. It seemed best to sit tight and wait.

I returned from the long drive calmer and more stoical in my attitude. But it was not to last.

CHAPTER THIRTEEN

The week-end was fine and I worked in the garden with a demoniac energy, my mother calling comments and suggestions from the terrace where she sat in her chair, swathed in rugs.

The indefatigable Daisy brought out gallons of coffee and delicious foods to keep up my strength. We ragged each other mercilessly.

Kate Hetherington came to see us on Sunday. She arrived in the antique open Rolls she loved to drive; a huge figure in a sheepskin coat, boots and a scarlet woollen cap.

'Good gracious, woman,' she said to Mother. 'What are you doing sitting in this damp air? It's getting too late for you to be out,' and, ignoring my mother's protests that she liked to watch me garden, she firmly pushed the wheel chair into the warm sitting-room.

Then she came striding around, examining my work critically.

'Glad you are able to use the plants,' she said. 'Even if it does mean digging out stuff to make room. A garden needs a face lift after a while, just as much as we do. Though I'm afraid mine's collapsed too far – it would need a couple of cranes to build it up again.' She laughed uproariously and I joined in politely, though I doubted there was much cause for merriment in having a ruined face. However, in spite of her double chins and sagging cheeks, her complexion was clear, her eyes sparkled, and her hair still held some of the red-gold lights of its original colour.

'I've brought some slides of Kenya to show your mother. She told me you had some too. So if you care to dig out the projector, we'll have a joint show.'

'Good idea, Kate. I'll finish putting in this azalea, then I'll join you.'

Daisy produced an enormous tea and we gathered round the log fire to devour it. There were piles of buttery crumpets, hot scones, toast, three kinds of jam and a home-baked cake. I drew the curtains, sank gratefully into an armchair and relaxed.

'Gracious, girl,' Kate said, 'what on earth have you got here? There's enough food to feed an army. And crumpets don't keep. Sheer extravagance.'

'Lady Hetherington,' Daisy said, 'I know your type. You act mean and are generous to a fault. Why don't you stop complaining and tuck in?'

Kate Hetherington, taken aback at Daisy's direct manner, was stunned into silence. Then she burst into a roar of laughter.

'You know, I like you, Daisy,' she said through her tears; she usually cried when she laughed. 'When you've had enough of these difficult people come and work for me. You can have a job any time.'

'Nothing doing,' I said firmly. 'Daisy stays.'

'Hear, hear,' Mother echoed.

Daisy glowed. 'Thank you, Lady Hetherington. Don't think I'm turning my nose up at the offer of a good job, but so long as they want me here, I'll stay. I just hate all that packing and unpacking.'

She withdrew to the kitchen tactfully to have her own tea. Although Daisy shared all meals companionably with my mother, she always effaced herself when there were visitors. Not from a sense of inferiority; just to avoid intruding on the intimate gossip of friends. She was a sensible and cosy woman and I became increasingly attached to her.

Later, she cleared away the tea things while I set up the projector and screen. Then she joined us to see the slides.

Kate's slides of Kenya were mainly of animals: lion, elephant, zebra, giraffe, and more and more elephants.

'Well, that's all I've brought,' Kate said finally. 'I'll bring some more next time.'

'Very interesting,' my mother commented. 'I do admire you for putting up with so much discomfort. I'm afraid I have to confine my animal studies to the London Zoo. Now, John, let's have a look at your travels.'

'I can't compete for excitement. Mine are just views. These are all of Rio. The ones I took in Peru haven't come back from the processers yet.'

There were one or two shots of Copacabana's crowded beaches, but most were taken from the top of Corcovado the day I had gone up to see the huge stone figure of Christ with Anita.

'What a fantastic view!' Kate said. 'Who's the pretty girl, John?' Anita was in one of the shots, smiling and waving.

'Which one?' I asked. 'They're all pretty,' and hurriedly changed the slide.

'There she is again,' Kate said. 'She's definitely smiling at you.'

Daisy came to my rescue. 'Why shouldn't she? I'd smile at him if I was a pretty girl.'

My mother said nothing. She never discussed my conquests. I cursed myself for my carelessness again and switched to some slides of the carnival at night, none of which were much good. I was reluctant to go on. There now flashed continuously in my inner eye the vision of

Anita: smiling, pouting, coquettish, flirting around in her bright fancy dress like a butterfly; then there she was suddenly: on the pavement, her head at an odd angle, blood oozing from her temple. I felt a brute – ashamed again and fearful. I became silent and put the slides away. I could not bear to go on talking about my travels.

'I must get back, Mother,' I said abruptly. 'I have to study a brief before tomorrow.'

Tearing back to London in the Porsche, I firmly made up my mind that, when the grey man rang again, I would tackle him and find out what he wanted. I was in the mood for a confrontation.

But the telephone did not ring that night, nor on Monday night. On Tuesday, while I was sitting down to a steak, it rang and I sprang to my feet, marched purposefully towards it and snatched up the receiver.

'Hallo, Devigne here,' I said harshly.

'Goodness, John,' said Rosemary's mild voice, 'what a brusque mood you are in! I rang to say Johnnie developed a slight temperature over the week-end, so I'm putting him back to bed for a few days. Could you postpone dinner till next week? Say Tuesday, unless you have a date?'

'No date. Of course that's OK. Sorry I was abrupt. I was deep in something else. You're not worried about Johnnie, are you?'

'No, not really. He'll soon be all right. He loves your mask and I have to take it away at night in case he falls asleep wearing it. 'Bye, then. See you next week.'

'Good-bye, Rosemary.'

I put the receiver down and mopped my face. The effort it had cost me to answer the phone was draining away, and relief taking its place.

In the weeks that followed, perhaps because I thought of him so obsessively, I saw the grey man everywhere. The weather was cold and rainy. It was the season for greyish raincoats, and many tall, gaunt men in London were wearing them. Just as I would catch my breath in anticipation, I saw each time that it was a stranger. As a result, I developed a kind of agoraphobia, refusing to go out to restaurants and avoiding public places as much as possible.

Fortunately, work continued to absorb me in the day, and clients were pleasantly surprised at the speed with which I progressed their affairs.

'A reformed character,' Edward teased, talking to Rosemary on one of the evenings I was dining with them. 'The easy-going John is now known to all as "Devigne the demon driver". Secretaries tremble and clerks cower at his approach.'

The evenings were more difficult. Apart from the one night a week I spent at Rosemary's, I sat at home listening to music or trying to read, finding it hard to concentrate, wondering whether the telephone would ring, my mind constantly drifting around my problems.

A part of me longed for a confrontation with the grey man. At times I brooded on black schemes. I had no revolver, but one day I looked speculatively at my long, lean fishing knife with the serrated edge; a deadly weapon. Standing in front of the hall mirror, I tried it against my body. Would I have the courage to lure the man up here and plunge into him? I made a wry face: all that gore and torn flesh! What on earth would I do with the body anyway? In books, murderers had it absolutely taped. They bumped off their victim, pushed the body into a cupboard, and later carried it down to the waiting car at dead of night. They usually disposed of it in a convenient ravine or wood. It sounded so easy.

Trying to picture myself acting out this sinister rôle, I laughed aloud. It was grotesque. And what a mess I would make of it! Even if I had been instrumental in the death of two girls, through accident rather than design, I was not an assassin and could never subscribe to pre-meditated murder. All the same, given the oppor-tunity . . .

When I could stand my thoughts no longer, I would get into the Porsche and drive her out of town into the night. We would roar through the silence, the headlights swiftly slicing the darkness ahead, my brain stimulated by the speed and necessity for absolute control. On my return, I would fall into an exhausted sleep, often to wake, sweating, after my horrific nightmare.

I lived in a sort of vacuum; tense, nervous, waiting – and I had taken to smoking incessantly again.

I think I was very near the edge of a breakdown.

CHAPTER FOURTEEN

'It's a dismal day,' Edward said, walking into my office. 'Let's have an early lunch together and cheer ourselves up.'

March was going out in full spate, roaring and raining. I looked a bit dubious, so Edward added quickly: 'I want to talk to you on the Robinson case. I thought of another loophole last night. Besides, if you go on working at this rate, we'll soon have to sack the staff and close down; there'll be nothing left for them to do.'

By the time we had found a taxi and arrived at our favourite restaurant in the Strand, it was no longer early. We sat down to have a drink while waiting for our table. Dripping business men were hurrying through the distant revolving door, thankful to get out of the squally weather. I gazed around at the crowds with my usual fixation, while Edward talked. Then of course I saw him: the tall, thin figure in a grey mackintosh, just pushing his way through the door.

I jumped to my feet with a cry, knocking my drink over the rickety table.

'What is it?' Edward beside me grasped my arm protectively.

'Nothing. I'm sorry. I though it was a man I did not particularly want to meet.' The familiar silhouette again had disclosed the face of a total stranger.

I was shaking. 'Here,' Edward said, pushing his

whisky towards me. 'Have mine.' And then he added quietly: 'John, don't you think it's time you told me all about it? You know I would stick by you and help, whatever your problems, real or imaginery.'

'Even murder?' I asked, before I could stop myself.

Edward looked grave. 'Even murder,' he said finally.

I looked at his kind, intelligent face. I could trust him. If I didn't unburden myself soon, I would surely crack.

'All right,' I said. 'I'll tell you, but not here. Let's grab a sandwich at the bar and go back to the privacy of our office.'

Once back there, we told the secretary we were in conference and not to put any calls through. Then we went into Edward's room and sat in the two armchairs, facing each other. I started to talk.

I had lived so long in silence on the subject of Maria although inside my mind there was a constant clamour, now it was a release to talk at last: mention her name, describe her. The words poured out. I told Edward everything.

When I came to the final scene, her spit on the carpet, I curled up with shame. I felt as she had felt; hatred for myself. I stopped talking. There was a silence.

Edward put the tips of his fingers together, as I had seen him do so often when advising a client. He was viewing my tale objectively.

'Rosemary was right,' Edward finally pronounced, 'in all but one thing. *"Cherchez la femme"*,' she said. She guessed you were in love at last, but she thought that the girl had jilted *you*. She reckoned you had been so spoilt, it was something you could not take. I see it goes much deeper than that. And Maria disappeared?'

'Without trace. We had no address; not one person who knew anything about her background – except possibly her previous employers, the Plummers. He was

136

posted to Mexico and that's why I went there. But I failed in that too. They were absent. I became convinced Maria had carried out her intention and done away with herself.'

'Not necessarily,' Edward said calmly. 'She may have aborted, or decided to go ahead and have the baby illegitimately. Lots of girls do now. We'll go on with that later. What really puzzles me, is why you came back from your trip in a far worse state of mind than when you left. You were anguished before, but now you seem tensed beyond reason, as though you are in what I can only describe as – the grip of fear. Why?'

I hesitated. 'That is another story,' I mumbled.

Edward leant forward and looked at me intently. 'But the key to your present problems. Why not give me the full picture, John? Get it off your chest.'

I heaved a great sigh and plunged into the saga of my travels. I explained about my obsessive certainty that the grey man was following me, how he kept cropping up in the most unusual places, how I felt I had at last escaped him in Rio. Then I described, briefly, the carnival and meeting Anita; taking her to the Opera Ball and there – the sudden reappearance of the grey man on the staircase.

'Like the phantom of the Opera,' I laughed grimly. 'It unnerved me completely. The noise, the heat, the crowds; I was in a highly nervous state and rushed away from it all with Anita at my heels.'

I went on to tell Edward about our quarrel, now Anita tore at my face; I showed him the faint remnants of the scar. 'And then I lashed out at her,' I said. 'I hit her and she slipped, knocking her head on an iron post as she fell down. I think I killed her. She looked terrible.' My brain flinched with pain as I said it and I made a physical grimace, closing my eyes for a minute to shut out the image. When I reopened them, Edward was looking

137

steadily at me.

'*Did* you kill her, John?' he asked.

I put my head in my hands. 'I don't know. I've been over and over the scene in my mind, trying to remember if she gave any sign of life. I can only remember her lopsided look, the whiteness of her face and the blood oozing down it. Just as I was about to go to her aid, I caught sight of the grey man at the end of the road, taking in the scene. I panicked and fled.'

'Maybe I would have done the same. Still, it was a damned silly thing to do. It turned you instantly into a guilty man. So you had a witness. That's a bit sinister.' Edward went into a brooding silence, pressing his finger-tips whitely against each other.

'I know you blame yourself for any harm that may have come to Maria, but however disgraceful your actions, they do not in any event constitute murder. The case of the other girl, however, is far more serious. *If* you killed her, *you* killed her – she did not kill herself. And you say you have a witness in this man. You really have got something to worry about there.' He was going on with his summary of the situation, but I interrupted him impatiently.

'I don't see it that way, Edward. Anita was an accident. She brought it partly on herself. Morally, I feel much more culpable over Maria. You cannot know how it diminishes you to feel the direct cause of death to someone you love profoundly. It strikes past sorrow to something deeper: the dismayed awareness of one's own ruthlessness. I know why Judas hanged himself. Sorrow combined with a shattering sense of worthlessness crushes the personality like – like one of those machines that crunch a big car into the size of a sardine tin.'

Edward gave a wry smile. 'Morally you may be right. Although we can't have you crunched like that, it must be bad for the digestion. We must try and uncrunch the Maria thing somehow. But legally, John, even if it was an accident, we will have a problem talking ourselves out of the death of other girl. Now, what about this "grey man", as you call him? Are you sure he's not just a figment of your overwrought imagination? Just another man, like the one you saw today?'

'No, Edward, no. He exists. I tell you he kept following me. At first I thought it might be a relative of Maria's, out for blood. Then I thought he was maybe a detective, hoping I should give him a lead. I did not know what to think. But he *was* there in Rio, at the Ball, and he did follow us and saw me with Anita at the end. He's a witness all right!'

'But why hadn't he reported it?'

'Look,' I said, 'I don't know what his game is. There have been two or three mysterious phone calls. I know he's around and that sooner or later he'll manifest himself. That's why I'm so jittery. I wish he *would* show up and declare his intentions.'

We stared at each other. I wondered what was going on in Edward's mind. Perhaps he had come round to the idea, which was also torturing me, that if I were arrested, the scandal could break the firm and Edward's own career would be in ruins. Perhaps I should resign right now.

Edward said thoughtfully, 'When he does show up, let me know and we'll confront him together. It could be blackmail.'

'It has been a relief telling you, Edward,' I said. 'Maybe I should have done so long ago. But there's absolutely no need for you to get involved. I think I should resign from the firm right away. Perhaps I'll buy a bit of land near Mother and grow things,' I finished vaguely.

Edward made an impatient gesture. 'Don't be a nit, John. Let's not meet trouble half way. You are in a frightful stew, and carrying the load on your own has got you down. The firm of Devigne and Drake has been a successful partnership and will go on that way, I hope, for a long time. Now I want to think over what you've told me; to sort out the real from the possible imaginery. You are bound to have got some of it out of proportion, in Maria's case particularly, because you feel so strongly about her. Will you mind if I tell Rosemary some of the tale of Maria? I won't mention the other girl for obvious reasons. But Rosie has been worried sick over you. She said yesterday: "Though John was never fat, he's positively skeletal now. He's in trouble. Can't we help?" When I told her you ate a sandwich at your office for lunch, she was horrified and made me promise to take you out and feed you up. Today was to be the first of a campaign. Yes, I think the tale of Maria could be told to her in part – if you'll allow it.'

'All right,' I said. 'But mind how you tell it. I value Rosemary's good opinion. I should hate her to cast me out.'

'Rely on me.' Edward smiled. 'By the way, your mother may be troubled about you too. She rang Rosie and asked us to come down one week-end soon. She said to fix it with you.'

'Did she now?' I was surprised. 'Well, that will be fun.' I looked at the calendar. 'Tomorrow it's April the first. Can you come the week-end after next?'

'I'll have to ask the management. I'm not sure how Rosie feels about travelling; she's in her fourth month, a tricky period. If she says it's OK, I'll probably take the two girls to stay with their granny and we'll bring Johnnie with us. Change of air will do him good.'

And so it was arranged. I felt much better after my confession. I thought what a lucky chap I was in some ways. Not many could boast a friend like Edward.

CHAPTER FIFTEEN

The Saturday morning I went to collect Rosemary was mild and sunny with the sudden warmth that sometimes comes in April. Edward had already left with the two little girls to take them to their granny. He was to join us later.

Rosemary was waiting, surrounded by the clobber that travels around with a three-year-old. Johnnie came funning at Rosemary's call, wearing the evil mask and making aggressive, growling noises behind it. As always, I recoiled from the wretched thing; it was too steeped in memories from which my mind shrank.

'Take that silly mask off, Johnnie,' I said, quite sharply. 'Give it back to me and I'll give you a car instead.'

Johnnie obediently took the mask off, but he put it firmly behind his back. 'It my mast,' he said. His little feet were planted squarely apart and he frowned with determination. In spite of his blond locks, he was a miniature Edward.

'All right.' I laughed. 'Have it your own way.' And I heaved him on to my shoulder and carried him to the Porsche.

As my car was not equipped with a baby seat at the back, Rosemary put Johnnie beside her in the front and the safety belt went over them both.

'Now remember you are driving for three and a half,'

she said. 'I hope you won't let us in for one of your trigger-happy speed jaunts. I think, on the whole, your mother would prefer to see us all alive.'

'Don't worry. I'll be careful.' Her words had stirred up memories and I became silent threading my way out of London, one half of my mind on the traffic, the other on Maria, as usual. It was about this time, on just such a lovely day, that I had first met her, only a year ago. It seemed like something that had happened in my far-off, carefree youth. I was a hundred years older and crumbling fast.

Once out of London, bowling along at an even pace, Rosemary broke the silence. Johnnie had dozed off with his head against her breast, the mask clutched in his hand.

'Edward told me about your girl,' she started carefully, 'and how it all went wrong. I know I've been bitchy to you in the past on the subject of your affairs, but I'm truly sorry about this one. I can see how fed-up you are; that it was the real thing, at last. And, John, stop me if I'm putting my nose in where it's not wanted, I don't want to probe if it hurts, but I would like to ask you one or two questions, just to see if I can help.'

'Probe away, Rosemary. Your help is always welcome.'

'Edward said the girl, Maria, became pregnant and you repudiated the child; she was so upset she claimed she would kill herself and you've felt responsible ever since. Is that it?'

'It is,' I said grimly, wincing at the bluntness of her résumé.

'But you've no actual proof of her death. On the other hand, you've not heard from her and don't know how to get in touch. That seems to me to be your real dilemma. You went to Mexico with the idea of sounding out the Plummers, but they were away. Now, why haven't you written to them since, asking if they can put you in touch?'

I was silent for a while thinking how to answer. I could not say: "Because I'm a possible murderer." Rosemary knew nothing of Anita and the grey man. Finally I said: 'I've thought so much about it and cannot make up my mind. Conscience doth make cowards of us all.'

'Oh, doth it,' Rosemary mocked. I suppose I was a bit pompous at times; that's what came of living alone – having no one to send you up now and again. My mother never noticed that I needed correction.

'Look, Rosemary,' I argued, 'even if I do succeed in contacting Maria, she may just tell me to push off. She has every right to. Surely if she's alive and still loves me, *she* will get in touch. Our child is due to be born about now.'

Rosemary said, 'Maybe she's thinking the same about you.'

'But how can *I* contact her? The Plummers may not know her address either.'

'By going to look for her in Greece,' Rosemary said promptly.

I shrugged hopelessly. 'A needle in a haystick. If I knew she were alive I would have a try. Yet what if she *did* kill herself? I would end up completely round the bend looking for a non-person. I'm more than half way there now.'

Rosemary pondered. 'She does not sound a suicide type, but then one never knows. A friend of mine, highly intelligent, did put her head in a gas oven over a love affair. But, John, why take this so hard? She was an adult, able to make her own decisions – however lousy your behaviour.'

'Yes, but this was the second time.' I explained about the Greek student. 'She had only just got over him, when she fell in love with me.'

'I see,' Rosemary said slowly. 'Let down again, and pretty desperate the second time! No wonder you are worried sick and blame yourself. I must say I never dreamt you had such a tender conscience.'

'Oh, I've just been a bastard all my life.'

'You were born with these damn good looks, and found sex only too easy in our permissive society. But there's nothing permissive about love; it's an all-consuming emotion, and the magic key to happiness, or the most profound misery. Some of the girls you captured so lightly must have been through hell. You seemed so unaware, uncaring. Maybe, in a way, this has been good for you; you've grown up.'

She lapsed into silence after this homily, then suddenly cried in a different tone: 'Whoa! Take it easy, John. Let's not discuss Maria any more while you are driving. It's too dangerous.' I had been getting faster and faster, worked up by our conversation.

I slowed down remembering Rosemary's condition. Also Johnnie had awakened and was grizzling a little. We drove steadily in the bright April sunshine and Rosemary chatted young John up and kept him amused. It was not long before we shot up the short drive to my mother's Tudor house, and stopped smoothly before the clematis-covered walls.

'Isn't that absolutely gorgeous?' Rosemary said, as she unstrapped herself and stepped out. She was gazing at a large magnolia tree, its waxen flowers pink against the pale blue sky. Gold-cupped daffodils and white narcissus shone amongst the green lawns. Trees were unfolding their leafy buds. A flowering cherry was in bloom and the smells of spring scented the air.

Rosemary took several deep breaths. 'It's my dream to own a cottage just one tenth as beautiful as this. But with

144

all the kiddywinks, we've had to wait and wait. Hallo, Daisy. Isn't the garden looking lovely?'

Daisy had come out to greet us and help with the luggage. 'Hallo, Mrs Drake. With John here doing his nut at week-ends, it's getting more like a blooming Kew Gardens every day. How's my boy?' She stooped and gave little Johnnie a hug. He put on his mask and growled, but let her take his hand and lead him into the house.

My mother never fussed over children but her face softened into lines of pleasure when she saw Johnnie.

'Goodness, why does he wear that horrible mask?' she said. 'It is a pity. He's such a handsome boy.'

'It's a carnival mask John brought from Rio and he's proud of it,' Rosemary said. 'Better to get rid of his aggressions growling behind that than pointing guns at people, as so many children do.'

'It's the telly,' Daisy said. 'Too much violence.'

'Thank goodness that was not a hazard when John was a little boy,' my mother said. 'Of course, we had a war – real violence all around us – but no television to exploit the horrors for the sadistic titillation of the public. Perhaps that's why I've never had any problems of violence with John. I don't believe he would hurt a fly.'

I would not meet Rosemary's eye. My mother was right about flies, I did not believe in heedlessly taking animal life; but I could push a girl to her death and drive another to suicide through brutal callousness. Feeling a hypocrite, I went out into the garden to look at my innocent flowers.

Edward arrived in time for lunch. The girls, left at their granny's house about thirty five miles away, were coming to tea with us on Sunday.

'I've got my slides from Peru at last,' I said. 'There has been a strike at the printers; the batch on Rio slipped through, these were held up.'

'Terrific,' Rosemary said. 'May we see them?'

'I can't wait,' Mother agreed.

So after one of Daisy's mammoth teas and when Johnnie had been put to bed, I got out the paraphernalia.

The first shots of Indians with their llamas were met with rapturous cries by the women.

'Their clothes are so trendy,' Rosemary was saying. 'Those coloured skirts would cost a fortune in a Chelsea boutique.'

'What sweet kids!' Daisy was wistful. She loved children.

A rather splendid shot of Machu Picchu came on the screen.

'What a fabulous place,' Rosemary said.

'That's Machu Picchu,' my mother explained. 'It was the last hide-out of the Incas, never found by the Spaniards. No one quite knows what became of them. When the place was discovered, not so many years ago, they found the bones of many women and children buried ceremoniously and one male skeleton still sitting on a stone seat. It was part of their religious tradition that all dead should be buried; so he must have been the last male survivor.'

I listened to my mother in amazement. 'How on earth do you know all this? Have you been reading it up?'

'No. I heard an interview on television. I learnt more in half an hour from this man who had been to South America than I've learnt from you in weeks. I've never met anyone more reluctant to talk of their travels than John,' my mother finished triumphantly.

'It sounds creepy,' Rosemary said. 'Who's that ghostly creature?' It was the picture of the grey man when he had walked into my camera vision, while I was photographing the Inca walls. The shot was blurred as a result of the drizzle and my shaking hands, I suppose. A wavering, shadowy figure just discernible against the Inca stones.

'It is the grey figure of a thin man,' Edward answered calmly. 'Isn't it, John?'

'What else?' I muttered.

My mother leant forward with interest. 'Just look at those Inca walls,' she was saying. 'Nothing to keep them together, no cement or anything, yet they've stood up all these hundreds of years, in spite of earthquakes.' She was holding forth at some length, but I was not listening. I was peering to see if I could remind myself again of the appearance of the grey man. I knew that Edward had jumped to the right conclusion and was also fixed in an intense stare. But no features were distinguishable. It was more of a shadow than a flesh and blood figure. Still, I was glad to have some proof, however nebulous, of the man's existence, to substantiate my story to Edward.

'Any more?' Rosemary asked, getting bored with my absent-minded study of the same slide.

'No, that's the lot,' I said, also thankful to bring this session to a close. As Mother had said: never could there have been a traveller more willing than I to forget his travels.

'Well, that was terrific.' Rosemary sighed. 'I wonder if we shall ever make it to such places?'

'Where travel is concerned, I think I've done my stint,' Mother took up. 'A lot of it can be very tiring and very uncomfortable. The water grotty, the food often worse. The weather usually too hot or too cold. There are long dreary waits at airports and stations. Just to name a few of the disadvantages. Nowadays I'm quite thankful to sit in comfort, looking at the excellent travel films on telly – and dream a little.'

Rosemary laughed. 'The dream is always so much

better than the reality. Nevertheless, we are all devils for punishment and prefer the excitement of personal adventure. Don't you agree, John?'

Edward interrupted. 'John must be sick of travel talk and there's a programme I'd like to see on telly, if I may, Mrs Devigne?'

So it was tactfully broken up by Edward and I sat brooding in silence through the tough, James-Bond type of spy story that he switched on. Why was I not more like that? I wondered. Why could I not use Karate, Judo or unarmed combat, knocking everyone for six; sailing fearlessly through the most sinister situations? The answer was simple. I was no James Bond. Just John Devigne. I knew nothing of unarmed combat, having had no training for a war. Perhaps I should have learnt and landed the grey man a neat chop, sending him tumbling down that mountain and out of my life. Instead, I had allowed his presence to swell into a huge enveloping cloud of menace, poisoning my thoughts and dominating my life.

Later, Edward and I went into my study to talk about him.

'You saw,' I said. 'He was standing there against the stones.'

'I don't doubt you,' Edward said. 'Though I could make nothing of his features, the shot was not at all clear. But I still have reservations about him. I can't see why he has not come forward. You've been back quite a while now.'

'Perhaps he's come to a sticky end. Nothing would please me more.'

Edward gave me a sharp look. 'What do you mean, John?' he asked sternly.

'Don't worry. I'm not your born assassin. I don't actually *enjoy* causing the death of people.'

'You're too hard on yourself, John,' Edward murmured. 'You've behaved more like a fool than a criminal. At the very worst, we can plead and get you off on manslaughter. Leave it to me. That's what solicitors are for, as you know only too well when you unscramble clients from their own troubles.'

'Yes, Edward, thank you,' I said with humility and a deep sadness; not for myself, I was almost past caring, but at the thought of the misery such a case would bring to Edward and Rosemary – and how it would break my mother's heart.

CHAPTER SIXTEEN

The next morning was fine again and, after an early lunch Edward went to fetch Jane and Helena at Mother's insistent request.

The two little girls burst into the house and greeted my mother with affectionate hugs; she seemed delighted. She had crocheted them all caps. Johnnie's was scarlet, with ear-flaps, and he put it on instantly, refusing to remove it even in the house.

Daisy had really gone to town on her tea party, and afterwards organized games in which she made us all join, mother and Johnnie too. She drew a comic donkey and we stuck the tail on blindfolded. Daisy was the ideal child entertainer: indefatigable and amusing.

Edward looked at his watch. 'Heavens, the time's gone so quickly. I must take the children home. School tomorrow.'

It was now nearly dusk.

Rosemary said, 'I haven't packed yet, so you go on.'

'Right,' Edward said. 'I'll give the girls some cocoa and pop them into bed. Will you come too, Johnnie?' But Johnnie put his hand through mine; I was his favourite for the moment.

'All right, faithless son, you stay with your adopted uncle. Come along, girls.'

The girls had put their new caps on and kissed my mother good-bye. She looked as pleased as Punch as she gazed after them. Her face was relaxed, younger. The afternoon's laughter had been a tonic for us all.

Rosemary, Johnnie and I drove back fast through that tricky half light before darkness. Both Rosemary and Johnnie were fidgety; she was over-tired from the afternoon's activities, Johnnie was over-excited. She found it more comfortable this time, she said, to strap herself in and hold, Johnnie on her knees. He had put his mask on again and, with Mother's scarlet cap, he looked the complete little devil.

'Could you make him take that mask off?' I groaned. 'I can see it out of the corner of my eye and I find it distracting.'

'You can hold it, but not wear it now,' she said to Johnnie, removing the mask. 'And stop jumping about. You are hurting your baby brother. The little brute is giving me enough trouble tonight without you adding to it.'

We were approaching a village and it was practically night, when it happened. I was slowing down fortunately, conforming to the speed limit, when one of the village dogs darted out of the hedge on to the road in front of us.

'Look out!' Rosemary shouted. Little Johnnie flung his arm up, startled, and hit my face with the mask, blinding me. As a driver, my reactions are quick and controlled and that's why, I suppose, we got off so lightly. I swerved to avoid the dog as I applied the brakes. We skidded to the right, jumped the side of the road and hit the bank. Even so, the jolt was terrific.

I was stunned momentarily with the shock. The lights and engine were off. I must have done it. There was a silence in the darkness of the car.

Rosemary was slumped forward, strained against the safety belt. 'Are you all right, Rosie?' my strange voice

151

was asking. There was no reply.

'Johnnie, Johnnie, where are you?' He had fallen at Rosemary's feet and a sudden frightened howl greeted my words. Thank God, Johnnie was safe!

'Wait, sweetie, don't cry,' I said, unstrapping myself and taking him on my knees. 'We've had an adventure and you are to be very brave and help me. Mummy's gone to sleep for a minute. Now you sit at the back while I try to get the car on to the road.' Johnnie did as he was told; he was too dazed to do otherwise.

I could not get out to help Rosemary as the door on my side was tight against the bank. I prayed that the car would start. I turned the ignition key. No response. Again and again, I tried. I had just decided I would squeeze through the sunshine roof and climb out that way, when the engine came to life. Carefully, I backed the car away; the steering seemed to be working. There was an unavoidable bump as I got her back on to the road. Rosemary groaned and the tight knot of fear in my stomach relaxed. She was alive.

'Rosie darling, are you all right? I'm trying to get out to come and help you, but the door on my side is jammed.' It was.

'I'm all right.' Rosemary groaned again. 'But junior here seems in trouble.' She patted her stomach.

'Listen, the Porsche has survived. I'll drive her into the village and get the police to call an ambulance.'

'No ambulance, please, John.' Rosemary sounded alarmed. 'I don't want to be stuck in some remote hospital. How long will it take to get home?'

'Traffic permitting, just under an hour.'

'Then drive on, *please*. I want my own doctor and to be with the family. I can hold on. Where's my Johnnie?'

'Sitting at the back. He's fine.' I was worried. 'Are you sure you should go on?' Not wasting any time I was

152

already on the move to the village. The lighted sign 'Police' was on the outskirts. I stopped the car.

'Look, Rosie, I'm going in all the same to ask them to ring through and warn Edward. He can have your doctor waiting with injections, or whatever.'

'That seems a good idea. But no ambulance to a remote cottage hospital. Promise?' Her voice sounded tearful and pleading.

'Ok,' I said, doubtfully. Now how to get out? It would have to be the roof after all. I stood on the top half of the seat and being thin, it was not too difficult. Johnnie had stopped crying and was wide-eyed at my antics. It was quite dark now and the street empty, so that no one witnessed this strange sight. I jumped down, opened the door on Rosemary's side, unstrapped her and eased her more comfortably into her seat. She bit her lip in trying not to cry out.

The carnival mask had dropped into the road as I opened the door. I put my heel viciously through it, crunching it to a pulp. I helped Johnnie out, thinking it best to take him with me.

'Mast trodded on. It is a pity,' he said quaintly and rubbed his fist in his eye.

'Don't cry, Johnnie. I'll buy you a nicer one,' I said briskly. 'Come and see the policeman now.'

The sergeant behind the desk was the stolid country type. Minutes were precious and perhaps I was too hurried for his slow intelligence. I said, 'My passenger is expecting a baby. We have had a slight accident and she is not feeling too well. No harm done apart from that. Would you be good enough to ring this number?' I was scribbling it on the back of my card. 'And say that Mrs Drake is on the way; would they please call her doctor so that he is there when she arrives. You may not get any reply at first, but you must keep trying.'

153

He looked at me as though I was talking Chinese, turning the card over slowly in his hand.

He said, 'Is it your wife who is expecting the baby?'

'No. She's not my wife. Her name is Mrs Drake.'

'Ah!' he said, as though he had caught me out. 'Is this your little boy?' Johnnie was standing quietly, dark circles of shock round his eyes, a pink lump swelling to the size of a golf ball on his forehead. He was not complaining, just staring, interested in his surroundings.

'It is his mother's boy,' I said idiotically. 'I am not married.'

'Ah,' he said again, meaningfully.

I was about to explode. 'Look, every minute counts and I must press on to London. Will you please do this for me?'

'If the lady is unwell,' he said logically, 'would it not be better to call an ambulance?'

It was obvious, but irritating in the circumstances. I was going to answer sharply, when fortunately someone of senior rank walked out of an inner room.

'What seems to be the trouble?' he asked.

'This gentleman has a lady in his car who is unwell. She is expecting a baby. She is not his wife.' It was as far as he had reached in his thinking. You could almost hear: 'Fast London lot', ticking over in his brain.

'Inspector,' I interrupted, 'speed is the essence. I have to get Mrs Drake back to her husband. She insists on going home and to her own doctor.' I explained rapidly that we had had a slight accident and what I wished them to do for me.

'It is understandable,' he said. 'Provided the car is safe to drive, you must make you own decision in the matter. We will endeavour to contact Mr Drake for you, Mr Devigne.'

This man was quick; he had taken in my name on the

card. Into my troubled mind intruded the thought: when my case comes up for trial, they will remember this and use it probably, as further evidence of irresponsibility. But I brushed these secondary issues aside. While I had been talking to the inspector, the stolid sergeant had opened a drawer and produced a large sweet for Johnnie, who was sucking it contentedly. I smiled at him. Old slow-but-sure was not a bad sort.

I ran out with Johnnie and looked at my damaged car. The door on my driving side had taken the brunt: the handle was twisted, almost off. Better leave it alone. I went round and opened the door on Rosemary's side.

'That's done. How are you feeling?'

'Bearing up – but let's go.' Her voice sounded tired.

I got Johnnie into the back and covered him with my coat. 'Have a sleep, Johnnie. We'll soon be home now.' I think he was glad to stretch out on the back seat and close his eyes.

The best way for me to get in, without disturbing Rosemary, was the roof again. I took a quick look to see if the police were about, then I was up, over and into my seat in a flash.

The next fifty minutes were grim. I drove carefully but fast. It was unavoidable. Every time I stopped at the lights, I chafed, and twice Rosemary moaned. I only spoke in answer to those moans. 'We're making good progress,' I said the first time. The second, I said: 'We're nearly there.' What other reassurance could I give? In fact, the traffic was not too bad. Johnnie, mercifully, slept.

Edward was waiting anxiously when we drew up. He was already by the car as I was doing the roof routine. He said nothing in his calm way, just opened the door on Rosemary's side, unstrapped her and she put her arms round his neck.

'Wait,' I said, jumping down. 'We'll make a chair and carry her in.'

The doctor had arrived just five minute before. He was a man in his fifties, rotund and reliable, and had known Rosemary since she was a child. 'Can you collect Johnnie?' I called out to him, as we carried Rosemary upstairs.

I left Edward with Rosemary and went back to help the doctor. We put Johnnie gently down on his bed. The doctor looked at his bruise and felt his pulse. 'There may be slight concussion,' he said. 'Don't undress or disturb him. Let him sleep on.' Then he went to Rosemary.

I took Johnnie's shoes off and loosened the belt round his woolly trousers. Then I tucked him into his blankets and crept out.

Edward was on the telephone; he was ordering an ambulance while the doctor was giving Rosemary an injection. Fifteen mintues later, Rosemary left the house again – on a stretcher.

The two girls had gone to bed obediently and after the day's excitements were blissfully asleep. There was no living-in help. Rosemary did not want it. She had a woman who came daily and various baby-sitters. I offered to stay in the house if Edward wanted to go to the hospital. But the doctor was firm.

'There is nothing you can do there,' he said. 'You know she is in good hands. I will see to things personally. You may ring and enquire as often as you like. Keep an eye on Johnnie.'

'He's right,' Edward said. 'Stay anyway, John, and have a drink. You look in a state of shock yourself.'

He poured out two big brandies and we sat quietly and drank them. I felt nothing – nothing at all. Neither thirst nor hunger, pain nor sorrow, just a sort of blank. If that meant I was in a state of shock, then I must have been.

After an hour, Edward got up to ring the hospital.

'Well?' I asked when he returned.

'They say she's "comfortable".'

'I'll bet!' I snorted.

We went to look at Johnnie. He was sleeping peacefully and Edward smoothed some antiseptic cream on the angry bump.

'It was a dog, you know,' I said suddenly. 'It ran across the car.' I had almost forgotten about the accident. This was the first explanation of any sort I had given to Edward.

'Why can't people keep their ruddy dogs at home?' Edward said fiercely. He asked no more about it. He hardly seemed interested. All his thoughts were concentrated on Rosemary. Mine were too, I suppose.

Every hour Edward made another of those frustrating calls. Around midnight the doctor rang him. This time we both ran to the telephone and I listened in on the extension.

Rosemary had lost the baby. They could not save it. She had had a bad haemorrhage, but they had given her a transfusion and now she was sleeping. The doctor was brisk. Edward must not worry. Rosemary had a strong constitution; she would recover. But she would have to stay in hospital for a while. Yes, Edward could visit her in the morning. No one else. She needed complete rest.

When he replaced the receiver, Edward sat by the phone for a moment and covered his eyes with his hand. I had a rush of returning feeling. Into the vacuum was pouring the memory of all that had happened, the full horror of my own responsibility in the matter. The tension was over, but the stress was just beginning to make itself felt.

'I'm sorry about the baby,' I said.

Edward made a dismissive gesture. 'Just so long as

Rosie is all right,' We went back into the sitting-room.

'Edward,' I insisted, 'I'm a jinks at present. The Furies are after me. It seems I just have to destroy.'

'I don't believe in mythological Furies,' Edward said. 'Though if they *do* exist, maybe they will be satisfied with the loss of our child and leave you alone now. No, I don't believe in such stuff.' He poured us both another drink, absent-mindedly, and sat down. 'But I do believe,' he went on slowly, 'that often in the lives of men, or women, there come periods of great trial when everything seems to go wrong. Their future life is shaped by the way they cope with the storm. It is the turning point; the deciding factor is not always obvious, and if it is, the choice is often difficult. Don't lose your courage, John. You are letting things get out of proportion because seemingly disastrous happenings have piled up too quickly in the trail of your first mistake.'

A reaction had set in, and we talked seriously till two in the morning, mainly about my problems. Edward was insistent that I should make more effort to trace Maria.

'You worry too much about this grey man,' he said a trifle impatiently. 'Where is he then?'

'I don't know, but he haunts me.'

'It is your conscience that haunts you,' Edward said. 'Perhaps they are synonymous.'

I was silent. *Touché.* I recognized a core of truth in this which had long troubled me.

All of a sudden I felt very tired, and very stiff. Edward must have noticed. 'Stay the night and keep me company,' he said. 'Then you can give me a hand with the girls in the morning.'

'I'd like to. I don't feel like climbing into my battered Porsche again.'

I made up the bed after a fashion in the ironing-cum-spare-bedroom and fell on to it thankfully.

The morning was a riot. I heard the two little girls chattering to Edward and reached out for my watch. An involuntary cry of pain escaped me. I was rigid; my right arm almost immovable. Carefully, I swung my legs out and stood up. At least I could stand and my left arm moved freely. That's all we need, I groaned, having me laid up too. I staggered into the guest bathroom and ran a hot bath. My body was covered in bruises. The bath shifted the pain enough to make it possible for me to put my clothes on – an agonizing performance. I shaved and fastened up buttons with my left hand. Tying my tie was a joke.

It was nearly eight o'clock. I could still hear the girls' excited chatter and Edward's deep voice. Presumably, he was helping them to get dressed.

'I'll go down and start breakfast,' I called.

'OK, John,' Edward shouted back.

He knew I was efficient in the kitchen and had no qualms about my producing an adequate breakfast for us all. But with a paralysed right hand and a body that could not bend or stretch, it was not the easiest of tasks.

Hot milk and toast, I thought. But I could not cut the bread. Edward would have to do that. The bottle top came off in my left hand, spilling milk on the floor. I put the milk on and then decided to make eggs and bacon. I tore the the the plastic paper round the bacon with my teeth, got that in the pan, then tried to break the eggs. Two fell on the floor; the other two went in the pan. A new cornflake box had to be opened. I put it between my legs and jabbed a knife into it. A flurry of cornflakes spread on the floor. Meanwhile, the milk had boiled over.

Edward and the girls came in just then and looked at the shambles in astonishment.

'Sorry,' I said. 'A bit clumsy this morning. I'll clear it up.' But I knew I could not bend that far down. 'Here – '

I passed a cloth to Helena – 'lend a hand.'

Edward said, 'Are you all right, John?'

'Stiff,' I said. 'It's nothing. Please cut the bread. My hand hurts a little.' It was not so much that it hurt – quite simply it did not function. 'How's Johnnie?'

'He seems OK. Not as bright as usual. The doctor will be calling round later. Mrs Collins comes in at nine and will look after him. I'll take the girls to school, then go on to see Rosemary. Can you hold the fort at the office? I'll be in later.'

'You stay with Rosemary as long as you like. Clients will understand. I'll deal with them.'

Somehow, we got through breakfast. Helena, who was seven years old, was helpful and took a mug of hot cocoa to Johnnie. The girls bustled about, feeling important, pleased I was there. They had not had time to miss their mother yet. They looked at my battered car and found it all a very exciting event. Gleefully, they skipped off to school with their father.

Mrs Collins arrived to take over Johnnie and I took a taxi to the office. It was pretty well hell getting in and out of it.

The constant frustration of being unable to use my right hand and the shooting pains in my back every time I moved, made it difficult to concentrate on client problems. When my secretary came in with some letters for me to sign and I found my grip on the pen too feeble, I almost gave up.

'You sign them for me,' I said. 'I've hurt my hand.'

Edward came in around midday. His face was strained. 'She's weak, hardly spoke and slept most of the time, but she said she wanted me there, so I stayed. I'll go again this evening for an hour or so, if you don't mind baby-sitting.' Then he took another look at me. 'You are not exactly a picture of health yourself. Let's go for a

160

steak presently.'

At the steak house, I was so busy trying to hide my pain from Edward, I did not, for the first time in weeks, think of looking around for the grey man. I had forgotten him. The merciful dispensation of a counter irritant.

Edward said, 'Rosemary spoke enough to tell me how the accident happened. She told me she lost her head and cried out, startling Johnnie, who hit you hard with the mask. She reckons you were blinded, but saved their lives with quick thinking.'

'All except the baby's,' I said bitterly.

'John, we insist you are not responsible, so for Heaven's sake stop taking it on yourself. I know how you must be feeling all the same. Where's Johnnie's mask, by the way? I couldn't make out what he was saying about it this morning.'

'I put my foot through the evil thing.'

'You *are* getting superstitious in your old age, Father William, with your Furies and your masks.' He smiled reassuringly.

'I must be careful not to spill the salt,' I said, smiling back.

No trouble with the salt, but when the steak arrived, I hadn't the strength to cut it. What a fool: I should never have ordered steak. I pushed it away. 'It's too tough,' I said. 'I'll have an omelette.'

Edward's eyes were watchful. 'You're hurt – badly. Why hide it? Please go and see a doctor this afternoon. You'll be no use if you are disabled and I need your help. I was hoping you'd come and stay for a few days. If you leave things too long it is sometimes impossible to put them right.'

'Like the baby,' I said. 'Had I made Rosemary go to hospital right away, they might have saved the baby.' It was what worried me most.

161

'Rosemary insisted on coming home and, once her mind is made up, it's useless to cross her.' He said it with pride. 'Here's the name and phone number of my physio. He's a miracle man.'

I capitulated. The miracle man looked at the X-rays that afternoon and said, 'You should go to bed for forty-eight hours.' Then went into technicalities. A couple of discs were out in the neck of my spine. All the pain came from there, pressing on nerves which rendered my hand useless. The shoulder was slightly sprained, and some of the ribs badly bruised.

'Bed is out of the question,' I said. 'I must stay on my feet. Can't you do something?'

In the end, he gave me a shot for the pain and a couple of violent tugs, this way and that. He put my arm in a sling and said, 'Come and see me tomorrow – same time.'

The miracle worked. The scene shifted from red hot knives to just a dull fire burning inside me, slowly cooking my back. It was almost cosy after the previous agony.

I went home and packed some clothes then took a taxi to Edward's home. Already nearly six o'clock, he was fretting to go to the hospital.

The Porsche had been taken away by my garage. They had no idea how long the repairs would take, they said: it depended on when they received the spares. There was a strike on at one of the works.

Helena and Jane were thrilled to see me again. They wanted to look at my bruises and gasped with pleasurable horror when they saw my blue-black ribs. It was easier now that the arm was in a sling; I didn't have to pretend any more. Johnnie was lying in bed with two pathetic black eyes and a bump all the shades of violet. The doctor had given him a sedative.

We muddled through the next few days. I was in

162

charge at the office in the morning while Edward visited Rosemary. Most afternoons I went to the miracle man. Somehow we managed to cook breakfasts and suppers, making a joke of my arm. The girls thought it all a lark and Mrs Collins was a great help.

After three days, Edward said, 'Rosemary would love to see you. She's really more like herself at last.' His face had brightened the last day. So that evening Edward took over the the children, while I went to see Rosemary.

Her coppery hair spread on the pillow, her face pale, she looked touchingly wan. I said, 'Rosie,' and kissed her, overcome.

'What a scrape we've been in, you and I,' she said. 'Your poor arm. Edward told me about that breakfast. I laughed till it hurt. Thank goodness Johnnie's bruising is not dangerous.'

'Your baby,' I said. 'You and Edward wanted it. If only – ' I was trying to say: if only it had not happened to two of the people I cherished most in the world.

Rosemary took my hand. 'Don't feel so badly. As Edward says, plenty more where that came from.'

I knew what an effort that flippancy must have cost her. It clutched at my heart. I wanted so much to make it up to her.

'Rosie,' I said, 'is there anything, anything at all I can do to make you happier?'

'Yes,' she said. 'Find your Maria, or another like her. I want to see you gay and debonair again,' and she pushed back a lock of hair from my forehead.

'No one else will do,' I said seriously. 'You see, I still love Maria too much to fall in love with anyone else – and without love, sex no longer interests me.'

She sighed. 'Yes, I feared that might be the case. Then we must hope Maria is still alive.' After a silence, she added: 'I hear the children dote on you. Well, it's very

cosy here. I think I'll stay and just let you men carry on.'
When it was time to go, I kissed her good-bye and she
said, 'Come and see me again if the children can spare
you, and *please* do something soon about Maria.'

I left Rosemary with a heavy heart. Yet her words this
time had stirred a response. I felt keenly that at least we
were both alive and we might so easily have been dead.
Rosemary, in due course, would try for another baby –
and I?

Next month I would be thirty-three, I thought.
Rosemary's insistence that I waste no more time found an
answering echo in my mind, and I knew the first healthy
prick of impatience with myself for my fears.

In fact, for four whole days I had not worried over
Anita or the grey man, and the nights were so painful that
when I slept under drugs, they were dreamless.

In the next two weeks, apart from a dull ache in the
region of my ribs, the pain almost left me; the fire in my
back gradually died down. Only my hand was slow in
regaining its potency, though I could at least now sign
my own letters, shakily.

Johnnie's bumps and bruises had faded. Best of all,
Rosemary was coming out of hospital on the Monday.

I prepared a casserole for her return, and that morning
firmly packed all my belongings and left Edward's
home. They would want to be alone on her first days
back.

My flat felt terribly empty. In the past I had always
walked into it with a sense of thankfulness. Its comfort,
and the beautiful things with which I had surrounded
myself, had seemed more than enough to make me content. Now I barely glanced at these inanimate objects. I
wanted the warmth of a living presence. I thought of

Edward and Rosemary with their lively, lovable children, and felt more than ever the void of loneliness. The urge to make some positive move about Maria had taken hold; I chafed at my helpless hand.

The traumatic experience of the accident had acted as a catalyst, jolting me out of the depressed half-life into which I had sunk. Anita and the grey man, tied together in that inhibiting knot of fear which had paralysed my initiative for so long, were pushed into an inner consciousness. Now I urgently wanted to send that letter, provided my hand was well enough to write it.

Walking restlessly into the bedroom, I looked at the sad face of the silver mask, gazing silently down. 'My darling darling,' I begged, 'if you are alive, please help me to find you.'

That night I had my sea dream, but it was different. The sea and sky, instead of turning black, had a golden blue haze, and Maria was standing on something – I'm not sure what – just smiling at me. I woke with a piercing sense of relief. Where had I heard that blue was the aura of happiness?

It was three o'clock in the morning, but I got out of bed, went straight to my desk, and without further hesitation forced myself to write a careful letter to Mrs Plummer. I read it through, satisfied: the writing was legible, if shaky.

On my way to the office in the morning, I made a special detour in order to airmail the letter to Mexico. I dropped it into the box with a sense of elation.

It stayed with me for several days.

CHAPTER SEVENTEEN

Rosemary was pouring me out a second cup of coffee. She still looked thin and wan, but we never discussed the baby again. We had just finished dinner and Edward had slipped out to get a client's signature on some documents.

Three weeks had gone by since my letter to the Plummers, but with no reply as yet. My anxieties were back, crowding in on me fast. I stirred my coffee, wondering what action to take next. Rosemary broke the silence.

'John, you've gone broody again. For a time I thought you had quite cheered up. Have you got anywhere in your quest for Maria?'

I shook my head. I had been fearful of telling her about the letter in case nothing came of it; in the event of good news, intending to spring it on her as a surprise.

Rosemary looked upset. 'I think you've lived too long with your ghosts! It's time you laid them.'

I smiled ruefully at her choice of words. Rosemary was with me a moment later. 'Well, I didn't quite mean that, but it's not such a bad idea either. *Have* you done anything about her?'

'I'll let you into a secret,' I said. 'About three weeks ago, I wrote to the Plummers, or rather Mrs Plummer personally.'

'And?'

'No reply.'

'It's possible they are away.'

'I suppose.' I turned aside not to show the uncertainty tormenting me; that the Plummers knew no more about Maria's whereabouts than I.

'There's a chance that the letter has gone astray,' Rosemary persisted. 'Don't you think you should follow it up?'

'I'll give it a little longer, then I will.'

'You'll let me know as soon as you hear, won't you? Even if it's bad news, don't despair. We'll work out some sort of plan. For a while, after you got over the accident thing, you were much brighter. Now, I don't know. You seem to be slipping again into the old melancholy. It just won't do,' she scolded, concerned for my happiness.

Edward came back and we dropped the subject.

At night I looked desperately at my silver mask, willing it to send me good news. Every morning I rushed to the door when I heard the plop of letters through the box. The sick disappointment each day grew harder to take.

Two more weeks went by in this way and my hopes were sinking fast. It was now June. The Porsche was back and my hand much better. This week-end at my mother's had been wet and cold. Driving to London in the continuous downpour, my thoughts went backwards and forwards with the monotonous swing of the windscreen wiper. Five weeks since I had written. Surely that gave Mrs Plummer time to have answered, even supposing she had been away. Of course posts were unreliable. Would it seem over-anxious if I wrote again? Should I go to Greece and start enquiries on the flimsy information I held? And what if Maria were no longer alive? How could I face her parents? But better to face them and know the truth. I had a Greek client who was wealthy, influential and a friend. Perhaps he would help me.

167

Wet and depressed, I opened my front door and trod on a scatter of letters. As I stopped to pick them up, I saw the airmail stamps from Mexico.

I flung my wet coat heedlessly on to the Chinese rug and fumbled clumsily to open the thin paper. Dropping into the nearest armchair, I read:

Dear Mr Devigne,

I am so sorry we missed you when you came to Mexico City. We should so have liked to meet you and get some news of Maria. All I know about her is that I had a card at Christmas from Crete. Fortunately I keep the cards for a while and I have looked it out. Apart from the usual good wishes, this is what she says: 'Have come home to Crete and am living with my parents now. Give my love to the children. I often think of you all.'

No more – no address. Funnily enough, I've never known her address in Crete. I believe the name of her father's hotel is either Acropolis or Apollon, I'm not sure. I know Crete is a large island, but remembering something Maria said once, I think the hotel is not far from Heraklion, the capital, and looks on to the sea. But I'm not very sure about that either. She used to talk about St Nicholas being a beautiful place and that we should go there some time for a holiday. Perhaps we will, one day. Well, if you wrote to both of the hotels I mentioned, it might just find her. So very sorry I cannot be more explicit and I hope you will be successful in contacting her.

We've been on tour with the children for almost a month and I asked the secretary to hold all personal mail as it would have been difficult to catch up with us. So please forgive my delay in answering. Should you be coming this way again, do let us know, as we would like to make sure of meeting you the next time.

Yours very sincerely,

She had signed it with an indecipherable signature.

It was a warm, kind letter. Maria had always spoken of them with affection. In a state of shock, I poured a whisky and lit a calming cigarette. Dazed, I found it hard to adjust to the message in the letter and sat down to re-read it. But the message was loud and clear: Maria had not committed suicide!

I don't know for how long I sat immobile, seemingly drained of emotion, light-headed, like someone coming out of a long illness. Then feelings started to flow in again; with a flash of wonder, I saw everything in the room glowing with a special brightness. I walked into my bedroom and looked at the mask – no longer sad to my eyes, it seemed to smile. I smiled back: she was alive, my darling, and I would find her and talk her into forgiving me.

For an hour I sat steeped in feverish thoughts, making plans. I was decided to go to Crete personally, and start the search there.

As to the unresolved menace of Anita and the grey man, I made a dismissive gesture with my hand, brushing it aside. Let it wait.

One of my clocks chimed ten: not too late to ring Rosemary, I remembered, jumping to my feet.

She answered the telephone. 'Rosie,' I said, my voice sounding strange, 'I've heard. Maria wrote to the Plummers at Christmas – so she is alive!'

'Oh, John!' she exclaimed softly, moved.

'But I don't really know her address. However, I have some clues and intend going to Crete to follow them up.' A new confidence surged through me now that the nagging fear that Maria had taken her life was no longer there to daunt me.

'You must go at once,' Rosemary said, with her usual impetuousness. 'Don't waste any more time, John.'

'I can't do quite that. I'll go in August.'

'Why, John? How can you bear to wait?'

'Because I have a number of cases that have to be dealt with before the Courts rise for the Long Vacation. I don't intend to leave my clients flat and let Edward cope with the muddle again. We have to consider the practice. Edward goes in July and I'll leave as soon as he is back. Now I know Maria is alive, I have something to build on. It's only a matter of a few more weeks.'

I had thought it all out carefully. I wanted plenty of time for the search; if I did not wait until after Edward's holiday, I would be under pressure. Also, though my hand was much better, I wanted to be one hundred per cent fit before setting out.

'I suppose so.' Rosemary still spoke doubtfully. 'Don't come back till you've found her.'

'I won't. Thank you, Rosie, for caring.' I said good-night and replaced the receiver, standing a moment by the telephone in sudden uncertainty. And what if she rejects me? How would I come back then?

One hurdle at a time, I told myself; and settled down again to my planning.

My mother had to be tackled next, or rather informed of my intentions. The ambivalence in my feelings towards her had grown. My protective love was still strong, but I had come to realize that over the years it had reached an unrealistic limit. It chafed me that even now I did not feel free to act as my heart dictated in case it should upset her. She would have to face the facts soon; my mind was made up. No point in worrying her, however, so far in advance of the time.

Meanwhile, I booked my plane for August 7th and informed my Greek friend of my intended visit. Alexis Coundris. He was going to be in Athens, he said, and was delighted at the prospect of showing me his beloved

170

Greece. He would have liked to take me over completely and arrange my programme for me. The Greeks are very hospitable as I knew from the past, and it could become difficult. I insisted as tactfully as possible that I wanted to stay in a hotel and that I was going on to Crete.

'You must stay in the new hotel there near St Nicholas,' he said. 'I know the proprietor – leave it to me. I'll see you get the best attention. You book your flight to Athens, I will do the rest.' As St Nicholas was the place mentioned in Mrs Plummer's letter and not far from Heraklion, I accepted his help gratefully.

The rest of June went by in a flash. We were so busy at the office, I hardly had time to think. I saw Edward and the family off the day they left for South Devon in early July. After that I lived in a state of suppressed excitement.

My hand had completely recovered and I was gardening again. Bursting to talk to someone about my plans, I took Daisy into my confidence one week-end.

'You'll be glad to hear, Daisy, that I've made up my mind to go after my girl,' I said. (I had fed her a little information about Maria). 'She's living in Greece – I think – and I'm going away in August on a search. Keep Mother amused; she may need cheering up. I haven't told her yet, by the way.'

'That's the best news I've heard in a long while.' Daisy beamed. 'Your mam will be all right – you underestimate her, and we get along fine together. Lady Hetherington came round the other day. You know what she said? She said, "The garden looks fabulous. You'd miss John if he ever got married." And your mam said: "What makes you think he'd give up gardening? Anyway, I've got Daisy."'

I laughed, but my misgivings over Mother were not dispelled.

July crawled by. Sometimes my fears crowded in on

me again: should Anita be dead, I knew only too well that the police would not easily drop the case and could catch up with me any time – in six months, a year, two even. I would push the uneasy thoughts down; nothing must stop me now.

I greeted Edward's return almost with rapture and went to see them the next evening. All the family were brown and relaxed after their month's holiday.

'Rosemary, you look your old self again,' I said, kissing her warmly. Helena and Jane danced around me and presented me proudly with sticks of rock they had bought out of their own pocket money. Johnnie gave me a stone he said was magic.

That night, I held Rosemary's hand as I said good-bye at the door.

'Only a few days left. I won't be seeing you again before I go. Wish me luck.'

'Off you go and come back *your* old self.' She smiled, squeezing my fingers. 'Not only luck you'll need, but courage. I'm counting on you.' She was almost as excited as I was.

In eight days I would be on my way; I would have to tell Mother the following week-end.

On the Sunday after tea, while Daisy was clearing up in the kitchen, it was my opportunity.

'Mother,' I said quietly. 'You know I'm going on holiday in a few days. I'm going to Crete.'

'Crete? Why Crete?' Her voice was shaky.

I got up and pretended to be busy returning a book to the shelves. My back was to her. I would not answer, and waited for her next question.

'Isn't there a lot of political unrest still in Greece?' she asked.

I rounded on her. 'What about it?' I snapped. 'Isn't there political unrest everywhere? And are we able to set our

172

own house in order? It seems a terrible world – most countries ruthless for power, and humanity steeped in the wrong values; greed, selfishness, cruelty. Maybe this chaotic struggle for survival is an inevitable pattern of life – I wouldn't know. I only know that my own life is in chaos – and I have to go to Crete.' My tirade had turned to a cry of despair. It was not usual for me to adopt this strident tone with my mother; my remarks to her were invariably couched in gentleness.

She was silent now, apparently sunk in thought. Her face was lowered, so that I could not see its expression. Presently she said in a cool, dry voice, 'Life can be very sweet and the world seem a beautiful place. It is when our personal problems get out of hand that everything turns sour.' She looked up at me and I was surprised that, in spite of her light tone, she had tears in her eyes. 'Come here, John,' she begged, indicating a stool beside her. 'Listen, darling, I know you have been miserable for a long time and I think you should realize that I *prefer* to see you happy.' She took both my hands in hers and shook them to emphasize her words. '*Go* to Crete,' she said, 'and I hope you find what you want there. But don't you dare come back without copies of the Cretan frescoes. Some of their designs would look very well in my new tapestry.' Then she pulled me close and kissed me, pressing her wet cheek for a moment against mine.

She had given her blessing, after her fashion.

CHAPTER EIGHTEEN

The heat struck me as I came out of the plane at Athens. Not far off, the sea was shimmering in the morning sun.

Bundled in and out of a bus and into the crowded airport building, I battled my was through Immigration, then to collect my luggage. It was the height of the tourist season and the crowds were staggering; foreign languages crackled around me. I heard French, German, Dutch, Swedish, apart from the usual English. The Tower of Babel had nothing on Athens airport.

My suitcase was practically the last to appear and I was speculating on the problems of securing a taxi in the midst of this frenzy, when I heard someone calling my name as I came through the final barrier.

I saw an attractive, sunburnt woman, smiling and waving at me. She wore a brief cotton frock and open-toed sandals, managing an air of chic. I was puzzled and she made an impatient gesture. Then I recognized her; it was the wife of Alexis, Mrs Coundris. The last time I had seen her was in my office, in the winter, and she had been wrapped in furs.

'Mrs Coundris.' I beamed. 'How marvellous to see you.'

'Welcome,' she said, standing on tiptoe to kiss me on the cheek. 'I thought I had missed you. The car is just outside.'

She was not very big behind the wheel, but drove like a

fiend while she chatted brightly.

'Alexis has asked that you excuse him as he has important meetings,' she said. 'So I come alone.'

'It is a very pleasant surprise,' I murmured. 'You should have let me take a taxi and not gone to all this trouble.'

'Not meet a visitor?' she exclaimed. 'You are in Greece, and we are so happy to see you.'

I was getting the Greek hospitality treatment and certainly appreciated it. I find it a great comfort to be met and taken over on arrival in a foreign country.

'I will bring you to your hotel,' she continued, in her not quite perfect English, 'and wait while you check into your room. Then you will come to lunch, I hope. Alexis expects you.'

To tell her I had eaten a snack lunch on the plane would have been tactless, so I accepted politely. 'Do you know if Alexis booked the plane for Crete and when it will be leaving?' I asked.

She looked at me quickly, with a flash of merry brown eyes. 'Alex will tell you. But you must keep a little time for us. He wants to take you to Spetsai. We go tomorrow.'

My heart sank a notch. Tomorrow was Saturday. I had wanted to go to Crete at once. Had he booked my plane?

The hotel they had chosen was of the stately Edwardian type. Mrs Coundris apologized for not being able to get me into one of the more modern ones. But I liked its tall ceilings and my immense bathroom, luxuries the new hotels could not afford.

She was sitting on a bar stool when I came down, half turned away from me, sipping a a fizzy drink. I stopped a moment and looked at her appraisingly: brown curly hair, slim, tanned, and with a youthful gaiety. Although she had the sophistication of a woman of forty, she looked thirty.

'Here I am, Mrs Coundris,' I said, walking up to her.

'Call me Louisa, John,' she said. 'We are not formal here. Let's go home for a drink, it is quieter.' And she slipped off the stool, leaving her unfinished fizz on the bar.

Driving through the heart of Athens, I felt oppressed by the tall new buildings, the crowded pavements and heavy traffic. It had changed a great deal since I had been here on a holiday with my mother, some fifteen years ago.

'I came to Athens while I was still an undergraduate,' I said. 'It was a relatively small town then. But how it's changed!'

'Changed to nothing but stink and noise,' she said. 'All this pollution is called – progress! If Alex did not have to be here for work, we would move out. That is why we go away every week-end and stay as long as Alex can manage. Most of Athens does the same.'

I kept silent. I did not want to seem ungracious so soon.

They had a penthouse flat a little way up the hill of Lycabetos, which overlooks the town. The main room was long, with just three very good pictures by modern artists on its pale grey walls. There were a couple of outstanding Greek bronzes; otherwise the furniture was plain and comfortable.

Through the big windows, which opened on to a terrace, one could see the surrounding mountains. The lowered blue-striped blinds took the sting out of the sun and gave a coolish look to this pleasing room.

I sank thankfully into a wide armchair, while my hostess went to get a drink out of the fridge.

Alexis came in around two o'clock. I was glad I had had that snack on the plane, after all. The maid who was cooking the meal did not appear in the least put out, obviously accustomed to these hours.

'How are you, my boy,' Alexis cried. He was only in his late forties, in spite of his avuncular manner. 'Welcome to Athens. Though this smelling town is no longer for welcoming. You will capture the spirit of Greece when you come to our island. We are going to Spetsai tomorrow. You will not deny us the pleasure of showing it to you, eh? There is beautiful bathing, beautiful fish and beautiful women. Sure you cannot resist the last.' He twinkled at his wife when he said it.

'Who can?' I smiled back. Alexis was a short, dark, powerful man, who moved like quicksilver; magnetic waves radiated from him. It was hard to say 'No' to so much charm and goodwill. It was, no doubt, the secret of his success.

'Look, Alex,' I said, fighting to keep my end up, 'you and Louisa are angels to welcome me like this and I would like very much to come and spend a week-end on your island home. But some other time. Please tell me: have you booked my hotel in Crete and the plane to take me there?'

'Relax, John,' he said, quite undaunted. 'The hotel owner is a friend. I told him to keep one of the best bungalows for you. He will, don't worry, even if it stay empty for a few days. The plane is easy.' He waved his hand dismissively. 'I have interests there. My secretary will find you a place anytime. Meanwhile, we take you out tonight and show you Athens a little. OK?'

'OK.' I smiled, relieved to have made even this somewhat indefinite progress. I was quite determined to leave for Crete tomorrow.

The home cooking was delicious. It was meat and rice wrapped in vine leaves, covered with a lemony sauce. One of their sons, a tall, handsome youth of twenty, dropped in for coffee. He subsequently drove me to my hotel.

The heat was still switched on pretty high and I rested in my air-conditioned room. I had been let off the hook for a few hours and was due to be picked up at nine o'clock. No one considered dining before ten in Athens, often much later.

Around five-thirty, I decided it was cool enough to go and re-visit the Acropolis. A little fearful of disillusion, I paid off the taxi and walked warily up the first of the steps through the Propylaea, or entrance. I stopped and the thrill I had felt as a boy of eighteen, was running through me again. The mountains were turning rose red in the evening light and the marble Parthenon glowed, floating above the ancient City, a monument to the spirit that had enriched the world over two thousand years ago: a civil-isation so prolific in beauty and wisdom that its scattered seeds were still flowering in our time. I walked back down the hill to the busy centre of town, soothed. I was beginning to unwind.

They took me to an open-air *taverna* in the old part of the town, the *Plaka.* It was about ten thirty by then and the restaurant was packed. Three guitarists played and sang sentimental songs with more gusto than talent. It was difficult to make conversation, but Alexis managed to talk and joke non-stop. He took over the ordering of our meal and went into the kitchen to make sure we had the best of everything.

The 'best' was very good; slices of a hake-like fish, pimentos stuffed with unknown delights, various salads; dishes kept arriving in bewildering profusion. Alexis insisted I try everything, so I was not sure in the end whether I was tasting fish, fowl or fudge.

I could have done without the guitarists, but the night air was pleasantly warm and the Athenian society filling this place, cheerful and relaxed. Another coil or two unwound inside me.

Louisa laughed a lot, but it was Alexis who dominated the scene. I wanted to bring her into the spotlight.

'It is difficult to believe you have a son of twenty,' I said. 'You hardly seem that age yourself.' It was true; in this light she looked like a young girl.

'She spoils him,' Alexis interrupted fiercely. 'I have sent our youngest son to Eton. The public school system in England is the best in the world for spoilt boys. It makes them tough. Greek mothers love too much their sons and ruin them – yes, yes, Louisa, you know it.'

And not only Greek mothers, I thought guiltily.

'I have a daughter, Sophia, who is older,' Louisa said calmly. 'She is twenty-three. She is in Spetsai – she likes to stay there all the time in summer.'

'A great beauty, my Sophie,' Alexis said proudly.

'Of course, he spoils *her*.' She smiled.

'Yes.' Alexis twinkled, sizing me up shrewdly. 'I think if you meet Sophie you will like her and you will not so much want to go to Crete. Spetsai is a lovely island. Why you do not stay with us this week-end and see?'

He was persuasive, and I sensed the trap about to close around me – the latest 'catch' for his beloved daughter. It was time to come clean.

'Alexis,' I said, 'I am going to Crete to look for some-one. Someone I met in London. I lost track of her but I intend to find her again. It is long overdue.'

His eyes flickered with disappointment and he was silent for a moment, but quickly recovered: 'Ah, *l'amour*,' he said. 'Then we must not keep you.'

I pressed on: 'Alexis, all the same I hope to come to your island home one day. I cannot see enough of Greece. You have a beautiful country.

He beamed, gratified. To praise his country to a Greek

is the highest compliment you can pay him. 'May I ask you,' he pursued, 'who is this girl you are so interested in?'

I decided to take him a little further into my confidence and explained about my difficulties in tracing Maria. I mentioned the names of the two hotels I had been given by Mrs Plummer.

'Look,' Alexis said briskly, already quite reconciled to the idea, 'I will help you.' He had too generous a spirit to bear a grudge for a minor disappointment. 'Take this card to Nicholakis at this Tourist Bureau in Heraklion. He will give you plenty information. In the morning I will telephone to say to him that you are coming. He is a friend.'

I was beginning to wonder if there was anyone of influence in Greece whom Alexis did not know.

Louisa, who had been following our conversation with interest, was looking at me smilingly. 'I am sorry you cannot come,' she said. 'I also would have enjoyed showing you our island.'

CHAPTER NINETEEN

Alexis had kept his word. I wasted no time on arrival in Crete and took a taxi straight from the airport to the Tourist Bureau in Heraklion, only some twenty minutes away. When I presented Alexis' card to the young man there, I found he was expecting me.

'Mr Coundris has telephoned this morning,' he said. 'Unfortunately Mr Nicholakis is gone to meet a foreign Minister who has just arrived, but I am his assistant and I have already some information for you.'

'Splendid,' I said, excited. 'Let's hear it.'

He produced a map of Crete and on it he had drawn five circles.

'These,' he explained, 'are the five hotels of the names you want, within a radius of one hundred and fifty kilometres from Heraklion. Three are called *Acropolis* and two *Apollon,* as you will see. I have written it on the map. I do not know the names of the proprietors. Anyway, the name you give is very usual here, like Smith in England. Also the hotels change hands and we have not always the correct names. Anyway, it is better that you take a taxi and visit the five hotels yourself. Like that you will know. I have only been here six months so I am not familiar with the people around. Anyway, you will find them friendly and they will help you.'

'You have been a great help yourself,' I said, surprised at his grasp of English. Except for the overworked 'anyway' and a fairly strong accent, he was pretty good. 'Have you been to England?'

'No. I learnt English at school in Athens,' he smiled.

'Good luck. Here is my card if you want any more help.'

'Thank you. I will let you know how I get on, anyway.' It was catching.

I came out feeling elated. I had made a promising start.

But I was handicapped by my ignorance of Greek.

'Can you speak English?' I asked the taxi driver, still patiently waiting with my suitcase.

'A leetle,' he said, and looked completely blank when I put a few questions. It was the extent of his knowledge. I decided to go to my hotel and elicit their help.

It was approximately a two-hour drive, the first part between gaunt and arid mountains. The sun struck blindingly on the newly-made road and, in addition to my dark glasses, I found a broad-brimmed peasant hat, given to me by Louisa, very comforting. She had driven me to the airport and, as a parting gesture, took the rough straw hat off her head and put it on mine. 'Take it, you will need it,' she had laughed, 'and may it bring you luck.'

Presently we left the main road and the bleak mountains were now replaced by fertile, wooded slopes, through which one caught glimpses of a very blue sea. By the time I had arrived at my hotel, I was longing for a swim in that tantalizing blueness.

My room was one of a series of small white bungalows built on the rocks, tight on the edge of a curving bay. I was delighted with it and, throwing off my sticky clothes, I quickly pulled on bathing trunks and dived straight in. The heat and tensions drained out of me as I swam in the clear unpolluted waters. Later, refreshed, I walked over to the main building to chat up one of the pretty girl receptionists.

I had explained already that I wanted an English-speaking taxi driver and she had promised me a certain 'Takis' by 5.30.

'He spik not very good Englis,' she said, 'but he is very proud that he had Englis decoration, because in the war he help the soldiers who were caught in Crete. He is very brave. You like him.'

The brave Takis appeared on the dot of 5.30. He was fat, round and jolly; somewhere in his early fifties. His taxi was an old rattle trap, but he seemed game enough and we bounced off together to the first of our unknown hotels, about half an hour's drive away. It was the only one near enough to tackle that day.

Takis did his best with conversation; after a few agonized attempts we lapsed into silence. I wondered how we were going to make out with my non-Greek and his impossible English. However, the receptionist had briefed him at my request, so that he was not wholly in the dark.

The road wound between mountains and sea, following the coastline all the way. Spent by the hot summer, the mountains here were brown, dried out; only now the slanting rays of the late sun transformed them, turning them to gold. They swept round the bay in a curve and beyond, on the purpling sea, lay more islands, mysterious in shadow, so that it was hard to tell where land ended and sea began.

This constant lovely blend of sky and sea and land, all drenched, glowing in the soft luminous light of Greece, never ceased to delight me. Even so, my mind stayed restlessly fixed on the coming interview with the first of our five hotels.

'Hotel', however, seemed altogether too grand a description when I saw it: an ugly box-like building, one storey high, with fly-blown tables and chairs set out on a mean little balcony. My heart sank. It looked more like a small-time restaurant, keeping just a few rooms vacant for letting during the season. Nevertheless, it proudly boasted the name *Hotel Acropolis* across its dreary front.

Takis and I walked over and sat down. They had no whisky, so I ordered an *ouzo* for us both. The waiter was fat and looked as fly-blown as the rest of the place. Takis started in on his enquiries in Greek.

I saw the waiter raise his eyes to heaven, which is the Greek for 'No.' More chat from Takis; more eyes inclined ever upwards. Finally Takis turned to me.

'He say this place sell to him month *Aprilios*. But not to him – to his father. He not know name of man has hotel before. But he has daughters, he say, sure.'

'Was one called Maria?'

The waiter understood me. 'Ne,' he said, which means 'yes'.

'Was she beautiful – *oréa*?' I asked.

The waiter made a nodding gesture and threw out his arms to indicate fatness.

Not my Maria, I thought; and yet, maybe, if she was having a baby?

'Takis, ask them what became of the previous owner. Does he know where he went in April – *Aprilios*?'

More frustrating Greek chat. Takis turned to me, worried. 'He think girl marry and Papa sell hotel and go – go far.' He made a wide gesture.

I was bewildered. Fat? Married? It just didn't sound right. 'Takis, please ask him for the name – to find out the name – of the previous owner. He must have it somewhere.'

After some more Greek, the waiter vanished. 'He go get his woman,' Takis said.

The wife appeared, as thin as her husband was fat, dressed in black, shrill but kindly.

She shrieked away in Greek to Takis and then disappeared again.

'What's happening?' I was dying a little.

'Woman say think girl not Maria – she Mirto. She – looking – now name father . . .' His English petered out. The effort was too much.

The woman came out triumphantly brandishing what looked like an old account book. She showed the name to Takis who read it out to me. It was not Maria's surname.

A big sigh of relief drained out of me. 'Here,' I said handing the woman a hundred-drachma note. 'Thank you very much. Please keep the change.' She shrilled her thanks after us as we left.

Once back in the taxi, I was quite cheerful. 'One off the list – still four to go. You did very well, Takis, thank you.' And I patted him on the shoulder. He beamed. I was so thankful that this false trail had turned out false after all.

It was quite dark when Takis dropped me off at my hotel and rattled away, promising to call for me at 10.30 the next morning. He had to have the taxi checked first, he said, as we were going to cover a fair mileage.

We had discussed our plans for the morrow with the pretty receptionist earlier and agreed the route. She had said, pointing to the map: 'Here, at the second hotel, you will not be far from Knossos, so Takis can take you to see it.' When I looked doubtful, she added sternly: 'Sure you cannot come to Crete and not visit Minoan Palace!' Takis had looked shocked, too. I could see how much it meant to them; it was a question of national pride. 'Naturally I intend to visit it,' I hastened to assure them, 'but *after* we've been to at least two of the hotels.' They smiled their approval.

Chaos reigned in the hotel lobby. Several hundred tourist 'groups' had just been unloaded from their coaches and the desk clerks were going up the wall. I fled

185

to the bar which was relatively quiet and ordered some sandwiches and a bottle of whisky to be sent to my bungalow right away. The crowded, noisy dining-room would be a nightmare.

Thankfully, I left the tumult behind and walked out into the night through the paved gardens to my peaceful bungalow. I sat on the terrace with a drink. It was warm; the sea, phosphorescent, lapped a few feet away. Lights twinkled round the bay from the other bungalows. There was no moon, but the stars were large, bright and numerous; the Milky Way spilled right into my terrace.

Munching my sandwiches, I gazed long at the stars, philosophizing. They do not reduce me (as some claim) to a sense of insignificance, a mere speck of dust in the limitless cosmos. On the contrary, I feel uplifted; made sharply aware that all things have a purpose, and man, given his almost infinite intelligence, is in a privileged position. Yet, our intellect had still not developed sufficient control over our aggression, and judging by the explosions of violence all over the world, we might well be heading for total destruction.

Perhaps, I mused, our society was even now emerging from relative primitiveness, and it might take many thousands of years before we evolved to a saner, sounder civilisation. Or perhaps man preferred to go on and on in this way, in savagery and selfishness, with the nobler spirits for ever struggled to show the light.

But I am not of the mettle to resolve the problems of the world and switched my musings to my own destiny, which was complex enough.

It seemed incredible to me now that I had behaved so abominably to Maria – and lost her. Steeped in egocentric complacency too long, she it was who shook me into a realization of what love meant, and only then had I come fully alive, acquiring a new dimension. To find her and be given another chance, was my only hope; she had become the focus of my existence and I longed for her with an intensity of feeling which grew daily.

I sat on, brooding over the old doubts: how would she react to the possibility that I had pushed some other girl to her death? I must tell her about it eventually. As for her parents – would they jump with joy over a man who had caused their daughter such deep misery?

Some of the hotel inmates, fearful of missing out on the beauty of the night, were swimming in the bay. Their splashing and laughter broke my concentration, and I went in to bed. I think I must have dropped off to sleep at once.

Daylight pouring through the slats woke me around 7.30 in the morning. The opalescent sea beckoned, and I dived in for a long swim. By the time I had lazily drifted back to the raft in the middle of the bay, the sun was well up; shading my eyes, I took in the scene on shore.

I saw the well-designed whitewashed bungalows, a limpid sea below them and a soft sweep of mountain behind. A sandy beach, green pines, a *taverna*-type restaurant perched on a higher rock overlooking the bay. A dream hotel in dream surroundings. Alexis had chosen well.

I swam ashore and ate a delicious breakfast of rolls and honey and hot coffee. By 10.30 I was standing impatiently at the front entrance and, five minutes later, Takis arrived.

The first of the two hotels we were investigating today was roughly a two-hours' drive away. I knew at once it was wrong, as it was inland, and I was quite sure, from all Maria had said, that their place had a view of the sea. Also it looked new, and indeed we learnt pretty rapidly that it had only been finished and put into use a year ago. Though *Apollon* was its name, Maria's parents did not

187

enter into this one at all. I decided to lunch here since it was nearly one o'clock and told Takis to pick me up at 2.30, allowing him time for a brief siesta.

Still three to go, I thought, my anxiety sharpening slightly.

Takis reappeared at 2.45, looking a little sheepish. 'Go water – benzini. Taxi too much drink,' and he made gobbling sounds: 'Maka the big POUF.' This time he threw his hands wide to indicate an explosion. Certainly it was hot enought for the poor old war horse to blow up if it was not fed and watered. 'We go now – long way – one, two-hour to hotel.'

It was a hot, airless drive but I was relieved to find that the sea had reappeared and we were making our way to the coast. The location was right.

This hotel was an *Acropolis*. It was a fair size, modern and quite close to the sea. A notice outside read:

<blockquote>
Man Spricht Deutch
Nous parlons Francais
English Spoken
</blockquote>

I said to Takis, 'All right. I can do this one,' and went in alone.

A blond woman in her forties was behind the reception desk. I thought: Blond? Maybe Maria's English mother.

'Good morning,' I started. 'Do you speak English?'

'Yes. Good morning. You have a reservation?' Her accent was not English.

'No. No reservation. Would you please tell me who runs this hotel?'

'Runs? You mean manages. I am manageress.'

'You are?' I pushed a little charm. 'Your English is very good. May I have a word with the proprietor?'

She looked puzzled. 'Mr Panopoulos is in Athens. But I can tell you what you want.'

She had, in fact, already told me. It was not Maria's

father.

'Thank you. Do you know anyone of this name who owns a hotel near here?' I showed her Maria's surname on a piece of paper.

'No,' she said, beginning to look impatient. 'I am here this season only and I am so busy always I have not the time to know anything about other hotels. Excuse me, please. There is a group arriving in an hour and I have still much to do.' She smiled, harassed. I thanked her and left.

I made the thumbs down sign to Takis as I walked back to the taxi.

He looked sympathetic. 'Knossos?' He suggested tentatively.

It was too late now to continue the search. The other hotels were a long way from here and I felt Takis and his taxi had taken enough punishment in the hot sun. Knossos was near at hand; it would please Takis, and I had promised my mother some copies of the frescoes. I might as well go and see what it was all about.

'All right,' I sighed resignedly. 'Let's go then.'

Takis took me to the palace of Knossos with a certain proprietory pride, then left me there to go and snooze in his taxi no doubt, until I was ready.

This vast and complicated palace had been the centre of a flourishing town some four thousand years ago: the kingdom of Minos. The sophisticated wall paintings were extraordinarily good: thin, elegant figures of men and women, fantastic birds, flowers and beasts, which could have been done by one of our own greats – a Picasso, Chagall, Modigliani. I was, in fact, staggered by the evidence everywhere of a surprisingly advanced civilization. No wonder my mother had shown such interest.

Even so, the atmosphere of this place oppressed me. It was sultry, and I felt shut in by the many narrow corridors leading in and out of the numerous rooms; the Greeks had named this intricate complex of passages the 'Labyrinth', meaning the inextricable, from which there is no issue.

Like my conscience, I brooded, standing a moment in the shade to light a cigarette; wherever I went, I stayed trapped in its dark depths. Maria was the magic key that could free me. Yet, what of Anita?

Depressed, I threw away my cigarette, and in the act of stamping it out, I saw a man emerge like a ghost from the gloom of a corridor. He was dressed in pale cotton slacks and an open necked blue shirt, but there was no mistaking the grey eyes that glittered in that sunburnt face.

This was no ghost.

After the first cold shock of recognition which had temporarily paralysed me, a burning rage possessed me. What was he doing here? If he was out to destroy me, then I would destroy him first. Yes, this time I would kill him.

I looked around for a weapon, but there was nothing – only the ancient stones that had lain there for thousands of years. Still, I was younger and stronger than he. There was not another soul to be seen – just the grey man and I.

Even as I hesitated, wondering what to do, he turned and melted back into the shadows. I knew then that I must not lose him; that I had to find out who he was.

The steps I stood on were smooth and slippery, worn with age. As I charged won them in angry pursuit, I fell heavily, gasping in agony; I had twisted my ankle, painfully.

CHAPTER TWENTY

Nothing broken, I thought, as I lay there, rubbing my leg. Gingerly I stood up and hobbled a few yards. Determined not to lose the grey man, I staggered on into the shadowy corridor. The fall had delayed me just enough to give him time to vanish again completely.

The corridor was long and dark and, once my eyes had got accustomed to the gloom, I saw that several narrower passages led out of it. Which to take?

The first led straight into a royal chamber with an alabaster throne, gleaming cold and empty.

Hurriedly returning to the main corridor, I took the next passage and went through a series of small cells, to find myself suddenly in the throne room again. In and out I staggered, now in one royal chamber, now in another, and twice more back in the throne room. I felt surrounded in the dark passages, hemmed in by malign presences, gloating over my predicament. The signs of splendour, the magnificent frescoes, no longer made an impression on my harassed mind. I realized I could wander round in circles like this for hours, while the grey man might by now be on his way to – anywhere!

My ankle was throbbing and I sat down on one of the innumerable steps and leant against a painted column, considering what to do. It was hot, hot and still, and I took off my peasant hat and fanned myself as I sat there, resting my head against the column, my eyes shut. When

I opened them, he was standing before me – nor more than a couple of yards away.

A flicker passed over his cold stare. 'Mr Devigne, I presume,' he said, in a flat toneless voice.

Had I not been so tensed, I would have laughed. As it was, I stared back angrily. 'You have the advantage,' I snapped. 'Who are *you*?' I wanted to stand threateningly before him, but my ankle kept me bound rather inadequately against the column.

He reached inside his hip pocket and with slow dignity flicked open his wallet and handed me a card. 'My name is Edmund Suter,' he said, in that flat voice.

On the card was printed his name and a London club, which gave me no clue, except that he was English. He was saying: 'It was high time we met. I have been trying to catch up with you over a long period.'

'And at last you've succeeded. But, in that case, why did you run away just now?'

'Run away?' He sounded puzzled. 'I see,' he added, looking at my hat. 'I did not recognize you in that. It is a long time since I've seen you.'

'It is indeed.' My voice was constricted with anger. 'What are you doing *here*?'

'Very much the same as you, I imagine. Studying the wonders of the Minoan civilization.'

That is no answer, I thought, and clinging obstinately to the idea that he may be a detective, I blurted out, '*Why* are you after me? Is it in connection with Maria?'

'Is that the name of the girl you left knocked out in Rio?' he asked.

Instantly my anger was replaced by the old familiar guilt and anxiety. He knew nothing of Maria – Anita was in his mind. I desperately wanted to hear what he had to say and nodded silently. What's in a name?

'I think I should perhaps ask why *you* then ran away?'

he said quietly.

I looked down from his steady stare. He held all the cards; I felt horribly ashamed. 'It was an accident,' I croaked. 'We quarrelled and she attacked me; I struck her harder than I meant and she slipped and hit her head. That's how it happened. Is she – was she . . .?' I stopped.

'She was not,' he said calmly. 'She was recovering when I left her. I guessed it was an accident and that you panicked, thinking she may be dead. I saw your eyes in the light of a street lamp, you see; they were – wild – fear-ful.' His penetrating gaze still fixed on me, he continued slowly, as if trying to make me understand: 'We had been to so many of the same places in South America it had created a bond, almost as though we knew each other well, and I felt impelled to contact you and put your mind at rest. When I got back to London I tried to telephone you, several times.'

I passed my hand over my face, by now completely bewildered. 'But how did you know me? I mean why were you following me in the first place?'

He inclined his head stiffly, 'I *was* following you,' he said, 'but only in your footsteps. Perhaps I owe you an explanation if you have the time?' Then he smiled, show-ing ill-kept, jagged teeth. They gave his face a human touch, redeeming its severity.

As I stared at him, I felt the first sweet reaction of relief; somewhere deep down, a nerve of anxiety had stopped nagging. Peace and gratitude were flooding through me.

In this state of euphoria, looking beyond the grey man, I saw the bright sun shining on a row of Greek amphoras, which had once held the wine that slaked the thirst of the inhabitants. It seemed, just now, like a very good idea.

'I have the time,' I smiled back, 'and want to hear all about it. But let's get out of this stuffy place and go and have a drink. I've hurt my ankle and have to sit down.'

He helped me up, and as I hobbled away from the ancient site, crowded with ghosts, I felt in some extraordinary way that they had been on my side after all. Perhaps the gods had judged me punished enough and decided to take a helpful hand in my destiny. I was burning to know what rôle the grey man had played in all this.

Looking at him, I realized that the description no longer fitted. His sunburnt face and open-necked shirt had transformed him into the conventional image of the relaxed holiday-maker. Greece suited him; his personality had mellowed and merged with the marble ruins, baked by centuries of hot sun. His light eyes now reflected the pleasure of a man at home in his environment.

We sat at a nearby café and my strange companion ordered a chilled white wine. It was a Cretan wine, he informed me, and in his opinion the best of the wines in Greece. It certainly tasted like nectar to my thirsty palate and I very quickly ordered another bottle.

'It's like this,' he was saying, relaxing in his chair. 'I had made a little money and decided to spend it on a visit to South America, but I had only a limited amount of time to spare: three weeks. As I walked into the travel agent's office, you were coming out. You did not notice me, but I had good reason to remember you. The agent told me you had just worked out a three weeks' tour, finishing with the carnival at Rio. To cut it short, I booked approximately the same tour, except that I substituted an Aztec temple for Acapulco. The carnival was a fixed date so we were bound to end up there together. I was very drawn to it; I wanted to witness a people still steeped in the carnival spirit. Of course, travel for me is not only a pleasure, but a necessary part of my work.'

He lapsed into silence and I waited. 'What is your

work?' I asked finally, impatiently.

'I am an anthropologist,' he said, looking a little surprised, as though I should have known. 'The study of man is my life's work.'

'An anthropologist! Of course, that's where I first saw you. At the museum in Mexico.' My brain was clearing of its preconceived notions and registering the true picture at long last.

'Yes.' He nodded. 'I recognized you there. You were fixed in my mind from then on. Once or twice I thought of approaching you, but you seemed almost apprehensive of such a meeting. I am a little shy myself.' He gave his jagged smile.

'Now I understand,' I said in wonder at this amazingly simple explanation. 'I wish you had spoken to me. It would have saved me quite a headache.'

'Why?' he asked, puzzled, but went straight on: 'In Rio, when I saw you at the Ball, I had made up my mind to come and talk to you. I wanted to get to know you and thought it might be my last chance. I waved and started down the stairs. By the time I had fought my way through, you were disappearing into the streets with the girl. Elated by the general excitement, I followed. I even called out once or twice, but you did not hear me. Fixed in my intention, I continued after you; perhaps I had drunk too much champagne.' (I smiled to myself: this austere man drunk?) 'You know the rest of the story,' he added. 'I realized my sudden appearance must have startled you and that I was partly responsible for your panic.'

I was embarrassed again: 'Did you follow me? I thought I heard footsteps.'

'No, I stayed with the girl. I massaged her feet and hands and she recovered consciousness. Eventually I helped her to a café, and explained that she had fallen and hurt herself. I speak a little Portuguese. The girl was dazed and said nothing. She just shook her head when I asked if she would like me to call the police. The wife of the café owner was sympathetic and I told them to be sure to advise a doctor in case of concussion; then I left, feeling my responsibility ended there.' He paused. 'All the same, your stricken look intruded on my thoughts, and back in London I contacted the Agency and obtained your phone number. I telephoned you several times, hoping to make an appointment; once or twice I thought somebody answered, then it cut off. I had to abandon the attempt as I was leaving for a European tour which lasted six weeks. On my return to London I tried again, almost nightly for a short while, but without success.'

That must have been the time I was staying with Edward. How responsible he was! I still felt horribly ashamed. 'I'm sorry you had so much trouble,' I mumbled. 'I was away from home.'

'I admit I became discouraged, particularly as I was swamped at the time with lectures and television interviews. I was travelling almost continuously all over England.'

'Interviews!' I cried, clapping my hand to my head. 'Of course. My mother saw a programme on television she found particularly interesting as it was on the places I had visited. She said that the man interviewed told her more in half an hour than I had done in weeks. I remember now. It was you?'

He nodded. 'It was a superficial talk, barely scratching the surface, but it was all that the time permitted. I'm glad she enjoyed it.' He said, in his stilted way. Though now we had finished our second bottle of wine we were both considerably more relaxed. 'You know,' he mused, 'whether by chance or design, I felt sure we were destined to meet again.'

'Strange, I sensed it too,' I muttered, ordering another

bottle of wine. 'What brings you to Greece then? Work?'

'No. I'm here on holiday. I love Greece and escape to the islands whenever I can spare the time and money. I'm leaving in two days. It is a lucky coincidence that we met today.'

Luck, I thought, comes in strange disguises. I had begun to feel almost affection for this dry, factual man. I poured us both another glass, finding no words to express my gratitude. It went too deep.

We were finishing our third bottle in a companionable silence, when Takis appeared, to collect me.

'Can I give you a lift?' I asked Suter, and told him the name of my hotel. 'It is about five kilometres from St Nicholas.'

'I know, I'm staying at St Nicholas,' he said, 'though not in a hotel. I usually stay with a family. That way I get to know the people and am well looked after.'

So we went back together. Over the two hours' drive I began to talk, to unburden myself. The wine helped.

'Look,' I started, 'we met by a lucky chance here – as you say, it may have been destined. On the other hand, you had abandoned your previous efforts to get in touch with me. But what if I had killed the girl? What then?'

'Then, of course, I would have acted differently: certainly I would have been adamant about contacting you to tell you the facts – and left it to your conscience.'

I laughed grimly. 'My conscience! It was already pretty tarnished!' An then, with a sense of release, I plunged into my own explanations, giving an edited version of my story to this extraordinary new friend.

He listened gravely, looking astonished when I told him I had thought he might be a detective or someone out to avenge Maria.

'You see,' I insisted, 'she had so completely disappeared, and I became absolutely convinced that I had driven her to her death.'

He gave a sharp nod. 'Hm. Guilt confused you. Now I understand many of the things that puzzled me; the tenseness I discerned in you; your unpredictable behaviour at the end.'

By the time I had brought him up to date on the information received from the Plummers which led to my being here now, he had become totally involved.

'May I see the map?' He asked. 'I know the area around here fairly well.'

I spread it out on our knees, indicating the circles. 'With these three hotels I've drawn a blank. These two are left to be explored.'

'They are a long way apart, but could both be visited in one day. Would you like me to come along and act as interpreter?'

I was impressed. 'Do you speak the language of *all* the countries you visit?'

'No, no. I speak about nine and of those only five well,' he said deprecatingly.

'Well, that certainly puts you in the dunces' class.' I laughed. 'I would very much appreciate your help, if you are sure it is not an intrusion on your holiday time.'

We had arrived at St Nicholas and Takis stopped to let Suter out.

'I suggest calling for you at 10.30 in the morning,' he said, ignoring my last comment. 'This would allow time for a bathe. Does that suit you?'

'Fine,' I agreed, and smiled to myself as I watched him walk away. I was becoming reconciled to the severe façade, acting as camouflage for the kindness beneath.

It was quite dark now and once back in my bungalow I removed my crumpled clothes and slipped into the silky black sea. My ankle was hot and swollen and the water blissfully cool. As I washed away the ancient dust and revelled in the feeling of release which Edmund Suter's news had brought me, I thought how Edward would chortle when I disclosed the truth about the 'grey man'.

Later, lying in bed, my ankle soothed, I considered again the reason for the sinister impact he had made on me at our earlier meetings. From the first, he had stirred up in my guilty mind a conversation I had once had with Maria.

We had been talking about village life in Crete. Maria was saying: 'They do not take things light there. They are a tough, proud lot and often deal with matters in their own fashion. When a local girl was made pregnant and the man refused to marry her, her three brothers went to his home and took him on, one at a time. I think they would have killed him had his mother not pleaded for his life.'

'They sound fierce,' I had said.

'They are, very, if roused. They don't revel in vendettas like the Mafia and normally live peacefully, respecting each other's property, but should a member of the family need protection, they certainly rally round.'

'And would they rally round if *you* needed protection?' I had asked, amused.

'I can look after myself,' she had answered. 'I would not want anyont to be troubled over me.'

So Maria sowed the seeds which later grew to such dark shapes in my overwrought imagination. After witnessing the Anita accident, the 'grey man' had, of course, seemed a more tangible menace – personifying my fears. Though, had he not appeared on the scene with such shock timing, no doubt I would have stopped to help Anita.

I found his presence here baffling; it held a mysterious significance for me. No longer sinister, I felt he yet had not acted out his rôle; surely he had been woven into my life for a purpose other than to set my mind at rest about Anita? I sensed keenly that the thread of fate which had led me to Knossos to meet him was part of a pattern, like my mother's tapestry, still to be completed.

Before dropping off to sleep I tried, as so often, to make telepathic contact with Maria – and that night I woke, having dreamt of something she had once said. Just a glimmer in my subconscious, but it seemed important. It was one of those maddening, fleeting, quickly fading impressions.

Frustrated, I gave up and slept restlessly till it was time for my morning swim. It was hard to contain my impatience until 10.30, when Suter arrived with Takis – on the dot. A punctual man.

The first of the two hotels today was one the way to Heraklion and faced the sea. It was an *Apollon*; a tall building, the biggest yet of those we had so far visited.

Though some of it was occupied, an additional wing was under construction. It looked like one of the new state-aided touristic hotels springing up along much of the coast of Greece.

We looked at each other silently and shook our heads.

'I'll go if you like,' Suter said. 'No need to strain your ankle. You never know.'

I sat in the taxi with Takis, vaguely hoping for a miracle.

There was no miracle. Edmund Suter came back, still shaking his head.

'State-owned,' he said shortly.

'Well, press on. Let's get to Heraklion for lunch, then we'll be half way to the other.'

We sat in a shady *taverna* in Heraklion, ploughing our way through a Moussaka, while Takis went off to seek out some cronies. Never had he had so much driving to do so continuously, he had confided to Suter. We had told him not to waste too much time and he was back obediently in an hour. Hopefully, we all set off in the heat of the afternoon, on the long drive to the village where the last of our five hotels was situated.

'Do you know whether there will be a view of the sea from there?' I asked Suter anxiously.

'I'm afraid I don't. The mountains so often screen it. But it is possible.'

We were driving now through vineyard country and prosperous-looking villages with well cultivated farms. There were fruit trees and vegetables of every kind to be seen. Grapes, strung on lines high off the ground, row upon row, were drying in the sun, turning to raisins. Except for the young girls in bright cotton dresses, the women were all in black. The fine-looking men, often tall and moustachioed, wore big leather boots with their trousers tucked in, Russian fashion. A fierce independence radiated from them; they were not the type to be pushed around.

'These people seem relaxed and quite prosperous to me,' I said to Suter. 'They appear untroubled by political problems.'

'They are more concerned with drought than politics,' he answered, 'and what price they will get for their crops. It is the sudden prosperity brought on by the great expansion of the tourist industry which is corrupting the peasants. They are turning their ploughshares into taxis and selling their farmlands for development.' He sighed. 'It is not possible, or even desirable, to stem the flood, but fortunately it will take a long time before the beauty of Greece is spoilt. There are a great many islands. I could show you places where time has hardly moved since ancient days.' He paused, then went on, obviously on a favourite subject: 'When you arrive as a visitor to one of these villages, they come running to greet you and ply you with questions and gifts; they will turn out of their bed for you and sleep on the floor themselves. To offer them money would be an insult. I have experienced it many times, but with the present tourist invasion, who knows how long it will last?' He was silent and after a while added: 'A pity that your mission and my work precludes my taking you to these tranquil places. "Eternal summer gilds them yet".'

I realized then that he was lonely. His long, hard stares in South America had been but hopeful overtures of friendship. In spite of his success in the scientific study of man, his personal relationships with his fellows were a failure. Not quite perhaps: a rapport had grown up between us. Trust had replaced the original hate and suspicion I had once nourished.

'Edmund,' I said, 'may I call you that? My name, as you know, is John.'

'Please do, John,' he said, inclining his head stiffly. He seemed pleased.

Takis said something to him and they spoke together in Greek. Edmund turned to me: 'Takis remembers that this village has a view of the sea – it will be looking out on the southern side of the island. We are not far now.'

I waited tense, silent, while Takis took a sharp turn left and then, suddenly, the village was there. At the same time, the blue of the sea burst into view through a break in the mountains.

We stopped at the *Acropolis Hotel* in the village square, a pleasant enough, unpretentious building, whitewashed in the usual way. A mass of purple bougainvillea grew up the wall and cascaded from a first-floor balcony. This seemed more like it.

'Who runs this place?' I asked Takis directly.

He spoke to one of the men sitting at a table outside, sipping his black coffee.

'Andreas,' the man answered. Was not this Maria's father's name? I could not be sure.

'Andreas who?' I asked.

'Yiannis' son,' the man answered. He understood me well.

Edmund smiled. 'They never use surnames. Let's go inside.'

It was cool in the big hallway which served also as a dining-room. A few tourists were sitting at tables, dawdling over their lunch, although it was almost four o'clock.

Edmund spoke to a girl clearing one of the tables. She had Maria's dark hair but none of her class.

Kyrios Andreas, the girl said, had gone to Heraklion, so had his missus. Yes, he had a daughter called Maria. No, there were no other members of the family here, except for yiayia – that was the grandmother.

My excitement subsided; I knew Maria's grandmothers were both dead.

She came out, a wrinkled, smiling old woman, dressed in the usual black.

Her son, Andreas, she confirmed, had run the hotel since her dear husband, Yiannis, had died, God rest his soul. She crossed herself. Edmund managed tactfully to extract the unknown surname from her. I knew already it was no good and would not be Maria's.

This time it was hard to mask my disappointment.

We went out into the hot street. A few people were sitting outside their houses, watching us curiously. A donkey, laden with crates of grapes, was being led slowly through the village. In the far distance the sea twinkled bluely. I had no heart for any of it.

Just as we were getting into the taxi, the yiayia came out carrying a box covered in vine leaves. She offered them to me, smiling. Underneath were several bunches of the small golden grapes, seedless and sweet, that I particularly enjoy Instinctively I reached for my wallet.

'No money,' Edmund said sharply. 'They are a gift. Just thank her.'

'*Efkaristo poli*,' I said, in my best Greek. I had picked up quite a few words by now.

The old girl went into her hotel, beaming.

In some way, this kindly gesture actually cheered me up. 'Never mind. Let's be off to the Tourist Bureau at Heraklion before they close,' I said to Takis, who was looking glum at the failure of our search.

'Well, John, I suppose you propose asking the Bureau if there are more hotels of the same name in other parts of the island?' Edmund was saying, as Takis started on the long journey back.

'That is plan B,' I said crisply.

'And what is plan C?' He smiled.

'A list of *all* hotels on the island. I intend to vet every one, however long it takes.'

'Good gracious! I admire your tenacity, but I don't envy you the job. It could be excessively long, tiring and frustrating.'

'Sooner or later I'm bound to find it. The trouble is, it will mean a great deal of travelling, and I wonder whether Takis can take it!'

Edmund laughed suddenly. It was a rare sound coming from him.

'You look so determined. This quest has quite changed your personality. I must say I envy you. You have hope. I have none.' He said it factually; in fact he had only just stopped laughing.

I looked at him with a new awareness. 'Are you married, Edmund?' I asked, curious.

'I was, long ago. My wife left me. It's an old story; not very pleasant.'

'What happened?' I felt he wanted to tell me.

'I don't think she ever loved me,' he said in his dry way. 'She married me because, I suppose, my profession held a certain glamour in her eyes – travel! But I was not so well established then and could not take her with me on all my lectures. I had been in Scotland for three days and when I came back, she was gone. We had been married almost exactly two years.' His face had become stern and he looked, for the moment, like the grey man I remembered.

'Shame,' I murmured.

'It was the manner of her leaving that was so destructive,' he continued, his eyes bleak. 'The house looked empty when I came in; the clock in the hall had gone. I went into the sitting-room: the armchairs, television set, all except a heavy dining-table and a chair, had gone. I went from room to room, calling her. Empty. I looked for a note, some sign. Upstairs in the bedroom, the bed was still made up, and when I looked in the cupboards my clothes were there, hers had gone. It dawned on me then that she had left and taken everything with her. At least I had a bed, a change of sheets and a couple of saucepans. It must have cost her quite an effort to leave those.'

'What a terrible story!'

'I found the note at last, in the bathroom. It said: "I am leaving because I do not love you and I cannot live a lie." That was all. But there was worse to follow.' He looked at me blankly. 'She had been to the bank and cleared our account of every penny. It was a joint account; naturally I had trusted her. Fortunately there was a cheque for fifty pounds in my pocket, a fee. It was *all* I had.' He paused and sighed deeply. 'Of course, I found she was living with a boy friend, with my furniture and on my money. So I had to divorce her.'

No wonder the poor chap had grown so grey and grim. I said, 'You are surely better off without her.'

'Yet I loved her,' he said simply. 'And perhaps I, too, had failed her in some way. Still, that was seven years ago. My work interests me, and I suppose achieving a measure of success is a form of compensation. It is, as far as human relationships go, that my confidence was effectively shattered. I have never felt able to form any close ties since.'

'It will come back,' I said, smiling at him.

'Yes,' he nodded, serious, 'I believe you are right. Already, becoming involved in your troubles has shaken me out of my own. The best way to forget one's problems is to immerse oneself in those of others; but never before has my interest been sufficiently aroused.'

We separated at Heraklion, he to gloat over the art treasures in the museum, while I went to tackle the Tourist Bureau.

The assistant had a wild look in his eye, and I saw instantly that I had walked into a crisis. I started to explain about the failures and asked whether I could see Mr Nicholakis this time. He took very little in, his mind fixed on his own problems. Two girls were talking loudly on the phone and he broke in to give them instructions in rapid Greek. They all sounded very excited.

'I am sorry, Mr Devigne,' he said apologetically. 'We have a group of three hundred Germans to send home tonight and one of the charter flights has been cancelled. Anyway, Nicholakis is at the airport trying to fix another plane. I may have to find them accommodation for tonight and anyway, all the hotels are full.'

The usual snarl-up, I thought. Poor chap. But I was not going to be put off entirely.

'Just five minutes of your attention, please. As the hotels you were kind enough to indicate were not the right ones, would you, as soon as you have the time, look to see if there are any more of the same name in other areas? Also, I would be obliged if you could let me have a list of all hotels on the island.'

'*All* hotels?' he said, running his hand through his hair. 'It will take time to get out a list. But, anyway, when these problems are over, I will do what I can. You are the friend of Mr Coundris and of course we will do what we can. Anyway, I will telephone your hotel early tomorrow morning.'

'Can I count on that?' I asked a little sternly. 'Is it a promise?'

'Promise, promise,' he said anxiously, listening to one of the girls on the phone.

I left them to their panic, and Takis and I went to collect Edmund

On the way back in the taxi, Edmund was pensive. I, too, was steeped in perplexed thoughts, so that it was a silent journey until just before our arrival in St Nicholas when Edmund broke the silence, speaking slowly.

'John, we may be barking up the wrong tree,' he said. 'The name of the hotel could be a false trail – Mrs Plummer was not at all sure. I've been thinking: it is the right *type* of hotel we should be looking for. Your Maria's parents are educated people, presumably with taste. It is, therefore, a small family-run hotel, catering exclusively for an appreciative clientèle which is perhaps what we should be after – and I think I know of such a place. It is not far from here; unfortunately I know not where exactly, or what it is called. A colleague stayed there about two years ago and I had lunch with him. It struck me at the time that, though I shun hotels whenever possible, this was the kind I would choose above others. I've been racking my brains all the way for the name of the place. Most aggravating! I think my landlady might help me, though; she knows the locality well as she's lived here since her childhood.' He stopped, then added hesitantly: 'I have to do my packing, but would you care to dine with me later tonight? There is a little *taverna* near St Nicholas where we can eat good fish.'

'Delighted,' I said, intrigued by his theory. It was arranged that Takis should pick me up around 8.30.

And it was later that evening that Edmund confirmed his brilliant contribution.

'As far as I can find out, I believe the name of the hotel to be *Delphi*,' he announced at once.

As he said it, a faint spark was struck again in my subconscious. Why, why? Something bothered me. I was strangely excited.

'Where is it?' I asked.

Edmund had invited Takis to sit and have an *ouzo* with us so that he might question him. Now they spoke together in Greek. Edmund turned to me animatedly, roused out of his usual calm. 'Takis says there is a hotel of that name on the way to Heraklion, not far from the sea, where he once took a client. He had some trouble finding it as it is out of the way and the road is not good. He reckons, though, he can find it again with a little effort. Now listen to this: he believes the owner's wife is English!'

'What's it like?' I questioned Takis.

'*Poli oréo*.' He opened his eyes in an exaggerated way, indicating his approval.

'Right,' I said. 'We go there on our way to Heraklion tomorrow. If your hunch turns out right, Edmund, and Takis finds it, tell him I will personally give him another decoration.'

Takis beamed and promised to do his best as he rose to leave us. It was agreed that he should take Edmund to the airport in the morning, first.

'It's OK by me,' I insisted. 'I had better wait for that phone call from the Tourist Bureau. Takis can have his midday nap and pick me up sharp at two thirty.'

And so it was agreed. Edmund and I had a pleasant meal that night in the little informal *taverna* by the sea. We drank plenty of Cretan wine and vowed eternal friendship. I had never seen him so relaxed. We parted with mutual regret.

'Thank you, Edmund, for all your help. If you've guessed right about the *Delphi*, you will, in effect, have found Maria for me. I wonder now, how I could have managed without you.'

'Nonsense.' He smiled. 'You have plenty of determination. Courage, too. You may need it, John,' he added warningly. Rosemary had said something of the sort, but I think he meant it differently.

He was hinting at the fear which gnawed intermittently at my mind: that when I did find Maria, she might yet reject me. This was the prospect that frightened me most.

CHAPTER TWENTY-ONE

Takis was there at 2.30, looking sleepy but resigned. We set off again in the hot afternoon sun to find the hotel.

I had spent a restless morning going for long swims to ease my tensions. By now the revolting pallor of my skin was transformed to a healthy brown.

The Bureau had rung at ten o'clock to say that the list would be ready for me this afternoon. Also they had found another *Acropolis Hotel* at the other end of the island. I felt no great interest in this information. My strange excitement over the *Delphi* persisted.

We had been driving for about an hour on the now familiar main road, when we branched off on to a secondary mountain route. We twisted and turned and Takis went slowly, muttering and shaking his head, looking for a sign.

I was the first to see it: a smallish, arrowed wooden board. I tapped for Takis to stop. It read:

DELPHI HOTEL (Apollon)

English Spoken.

My heart gave a tremendous jolt. This had to be it. I got out feeling that dryness in the throat, a mixture of excitement and nerves.

I said to the ever-eager Takis, 'Wait for me here, please. They speak English.'

He nodded thankfully, settling back into his taxi for a nap.

The arrow pointed down a lane, a few minutes' walk to the actual grounds of the hotel. Lizards darted under the hot stones at my approach, the light shimmered in the heat, and the loud chirping of the cicadas drowned all other sounds.

Once arrived at the wrought-iron gate leading into the private grounds, I was immediately aware that here, in the long border facing me, was the hand of a true gardener. Someone who cared had planned the large variety of bushes and trees. I noticed hibiscus, fuschia and geraniums flowering between silver-leaved shrubs. There was an English touch about the clumps of white and yellow daisies and spiky blue lavenders. This, I thought, is the work of Maria's mother. The English create gardens the world over.

This mass of colour was hedged in with Cyprus which ended in a clipped arch. Once through the arch, the house and its view were suddenly revealed. I stopped in stunned appreciation, forgetting for a moment the purpose of my visit.

On my left was a long, fairly low, two-storied building, L-shaped; its roof of rose red pantiles, its walls painted a pale pink, and the shutters a dark grey. A cobbled yard, the greyish stones set in mosaic patterning, covered the entire area immediately in front of the house. Several small lemon trees in tubs glowed against the pink walls.

On my right, an olive grove sloped steeply down to the sea, about five hundred yards away, and there is no view more soothing than the unbroken silver-green of olives against a luminous sea. From the blue unclouded sky flowed the clear light of Greece and for a moment I felt suspended in a timeless world. Had I come out of the past into the present? Or was I in the past? Gazing at the ageless, eternal, supremely beautiful scene, the spark in my subconscious flared, illuminating Maria's words. She had said: 'My mother was thrilled with the view from our hotel. She though it had the serenity of Delphi.'

So – they had decided to change its name!

Apart from the cicadas, it was absolutely still and many of the shutters were closed. I looked at my watch: only 3.30. Siesta would not be over for at least another half hour.

At the end of the short L of the house, vines covered an arbour and wrought-iron tables and chairs glimmered whitely under the dark leaves. I limped over – my ankle swelled up in the heat – and, taking off my peasant hat, sat in the shade. I would wait here awhile quietly until the household stirred. It struck me that this hotel with is sophisticated simplicity and well-tended look was, indeed, as Suter had suggested, catering for an exclusive clientèle. Certainly it seemed the sort of place I always hoped to discover for myself.

If Maria *had* moved on since Christmas, I could still talk to her parents and find out where she had gone. What exactly I would say was a blank in my mind. So many conversations rehearsed, that I could remember none. In the end I would probably tell the plain truth. I was past dissimulation.

Sunk in thought, I did not hear her come up behind me. She moved round to face me. 'John!' She said it softly, in wonder, her eyes widening in the remembered way.

She was still so beautiful, though thinner – too thin. Her face, too, looked older; there were lines of strain. Some of the innocence and freshness had gone. But I felt nothing but an overwhelming love as I gazed back at her. It did not matter to me how she looked. I would always love her.

'Maria,' I said, getting up, not touching her, suddenly

shy. 'Sit down a minute. I've come a long way to talk to you.'

She sat down like a somnambulist.

I sat too. 'First, I am so thankful to see you. What about our baby though?'

'*Our* baby,' she said, cynically. 'I got rid of it, of course. It is not a permissive society here, whatever that may mean. It would have been an embarrassment to my parents in these surroundings. And I could not see how to bring up a child on my own in England. It did not seem much of a prospect for the child.' She shrugged. 'It was not so difficult in the end. I was fortunate to find a sympathetic doctor. But all that is past. Why bring it up now?'

My stomach was churning with unhappiness. 'I'm sorry, Maria. Very sorry. I want you to believe me, even if you find it hard to forgive. I came here to ask you if you would consider marrying me. I know I behaved appallingly – well, I can't find the right word; but I regret it, bitterly, and I will try and make it up to you.'

I realized I was stilted, hopeless. We stared at each other – almost like strangers. This was not at all as I had dreamt our reunion would go. Where were all those words I had burned to tell her? How wretched I had been without her, how I longed for her forgiveness, how much I loved and needed her. I sat there, tongue-tied.

Maria never rushed in with empty phrases to try and fill the silence. Now it grew between us, as she considered what I had come to say. Looking beyond me at the house, her thoughts seemed directed to those inside it. At last she turned to me, her clear eyes puzzled – there seemed to be a question in them.

'Thank you, John,' she said, 'for coming all this way to ask me. In time, I did forgive you – or rather I understood your pressures, you see. I wanted to die at first; it was a

213

black period; then I got over it. The happy times came crowding more and more into my mind – and the bitterness gradually faded. But marriage?' She shook her head. 'I've promised to marry Costa. We are engaged.' She showed me a ring.

'Who is Costa?' All my half-acknowledged fears rushed in, jeering. I felt sick.

'He is my father's right-hand man. My parents would like me to marry him so that we can run the hotel together, later on.'

'I see. Another of these arranged marriages?'

'That's how it goes,' she said, with a false cheerfulness.

'And when did this happen?'

'A month or so ago,' she answered quietly.

'I see,' I said again. Rosemary had been right, after all. I should not have hesitated, wasted time. Had I come earlier, this might have been averted.

'You left no address. I had many problems,' I muttered. 'So many things I didn't know. Well – I've found you . . .' My voice trailed off.

She did not answer. Then she said, in that quiet voice, 'We are to be married at Christmas.'

So this was it. At least I had told her I was sorry; at least she knew that. I sat on, dazed with shock.

Maria waited quietly. This is how I had so often remembered her: composed, poised – gentle outwardly, with an inner strength and a great control. The only sign of stress she now gave was in the nervous twisting of her engagement ring. I watched, mesmerized, her slim fingers playing with that hateful object.

After a while, I thought: What am I doing still sitting here foolishly – unwanted? Though there was something else I had come for. What was it? Ah, yes, I had not spoken to her parents. Well, of course, it was no longer necessary. I rose wearily.

'Goodbye, Maria. Be happy.' Suddenly I remembered something else. 'Oh, I brought you this,' I said, producing the silver mesh necklace set with citrine stones.

She looked at it, then up at me, amazed. 'But, John, it's simply lovely. I can't accept it. It looks too valuable. Where did you get it?'

'Mexico, I think. It could have been Peru. I went away to forget you, but you were with me all the time. I think I became a little mad after you left. Keep it as a wedding present.' I stared at her a moment longer in that inhibited silence, then managed a smile. 'Good luck,' I said, and limped away, under the arch and down the long border ablaze with flowers. I saw nothing. Tonight I would book a plane for my return. Pointless to stay – all pointless. The road ahead was desolate and led to nowhere.

I heard footsteps behind me and her voice calling, 'John, John.'

I stopped, my stomach churning again.

She came running up to me. 'Your hat,' she said. 'You left it on the table.' Her eyes were unnaturally bright. 'And why are you limping?' She added. Was there anxiety in the question? As I looked into her troubled eyes, something at last unfroze in me and the words came pouring out.

'Maria,' I said. 'I want you to know I love you more than anything in the world. It does not come easily for me to say this; I've had no practice. You are the only person I have said it to in my whole life.'

She came nearer, crushing my hat against her body, her eyes still fixed on mine. 'I felt like that about you once. I thought I had got over it –stifled my feelings away – but perhaps I haven't. Perhaps it would not be fair to marry Costa if I haven't. It hurt to watch you limp – limp off like that, you see.'

'Maria,' I said again, 'I love you.'

She gave a great sigh and held out my hat to me absently. 'How can I,' she said, almost to herself, 'let them all down? Except – my younger sister *is* rather fond of Costa, and they could run the hotel together just as well.' She focused back on me. 'Why are you limping?'

'It's not serious. I fell and twisted my ankle.'

'There is still something you have not told me – what about your mother?'

'My mother knows. She knows, and has given her blessing.'

'I see,' she said, absent again, gazing past me, a little frown between her eyes. 'This doesn't seem quite real to me, you know. I dreamt for so long that it might happen; that you would miss me and come and tell me that you loved me. The feeling was so strong at times I would scan the horizon, like Sister Anne of the fairy tale. I *could* not write to plead with you – my pride stopped me. Though I told myself again and again that I was a fool, that had you loved me you would not have let me go in the first place. For months I resisted the pressure to marry Costa. And now, it's – too late. Why did you take so long?' The frown had deepened as she looked at me, her eyes blurred with tears.

How could I explain here, on this path in the hot sun, the twisted skein of events that had followed her departure – the way my conscience had reacted and the strange part played by the 'grey man' in the plan of things.

'It would take too long to explain, but I will tell you everything one day, if you give me the chance. It's not too late, darling, please believe me. I've suffered too – it's changed me. I took a good look at myself and didn't like what I saw.' I came nearer, still without touching her, my voice urgent. 'Maria, stay with me. I will take care of you, make you happy. You don't love this man. Maria. Don't – please don't – it would be a mistake. I love you.'

The longing to hold her dear self against me, kiss her, convince her, was suffocating. I fought it, sensing the timing to be wrong.

She put her hands on my shoulders. Tears trickled unheeded down her cheeks. 'You could be right, John, but I have to think. My sister and Costa have known each other a long time, and it *might* make her happy if I did not marry him. I'm not sure. I just have to think,' she repeated.

'I'll wait. I'm in a hotel not far from here and will ring you every day until you've made up your mind. I'll wait forever if necessary.'

For the first time she smiled and the strain went out of her face. 'I don't believe "forever" would suit my sister,' she said. 'You'd better go now. I'm too mixed up to think straight.' Her grip had tightened on my shoulders as she gazed intently at me, and for a moment, I thought she was going to kiss me. Then she smiled, with great sweetness, dropped her arms and turned away.

'Maria!' I reached out to pull her back, but she held up the palm of her hand in a stopping gesture.

'Not now, John,' she said firmly. 'Call me.' And walked quickly back in the direction of the house.

At those two words joy exploded in me, at last. Maria was not a tease. If she said, 'Call me,' she meant it. She intended to find a way.

I took a deep breath, filling my lungs with the scented air, closing my eyes. When I opened them, everything was shining, reborn: the flowers, the luminous sky, the gold-green sea; even the cicadas were singing in ecstasy. It was a wonderful world.

'Takis, you've won that decoration!' I shouted crazily, and, forgetting my ankle, started running in bounds towards the waiting taxi.